About the Author

Marika, from her earliest memory, has been a dreamer and a reader who has enjoyed the work of great and less great authors of fiction, with a passion for stories of adventure and romance, overcoming challenges and achieving the greatest expectations. She has been a writer, teacher, psychologist, wife, mother and hopefully a friend to those who needed one. Being able to write this book is the fulfilment of a long-held desire to write a story that could bring happiness to other enthusiasts of living and loving – people who take time, apart from the madding crowd, to dream and to hope.

When the Unexpected Happens

Marika George

When the Unexpected Happens

Vanguard Press

VANGUARD PAPERBACK

© Copyright 2025
Marika George

The right of Marika George to be identified as author of
this work has been asserted by her in accordance with the
Copyright, Designs and Patents Act 1988.

All Rights Reserved

No reproduction, copy or transmission of this publication
may be made without written permission.
No paragraph of this publication may be reproduced,
copied or transmitted save with the written permission of the publisher, or in
accordance with the provisions
of the Copyright Act 1956 (as amended).

Any person who commits any unauthorised act in relation to this publication
may be liable to criminal prosecution and civil claims for damages.

A CIP catalogue record for this title is available from the British Library.

ISBN 978-1-83671-015-8

This is a work of fiction. Names, characters, businesses, places, events and
incidents are either the products of the author's imagination or used in a
fictitious manner. Any resemblance to actual persons, living or dead, or actual
events is purely coincidental.

Vanguard Press is an imprint of
Pegasus Elliot Mackenzie Publishers Ltd.
www.pegasuspublishers.com

First Published in 2025

Vanguard Press
Sheraton House Castle Park
Cambridge England

Printed & Bound in Great Britain

Dedication

To my family who encouraged me to write.

Acknowledgements

My first book has been long in coming, but something I knew I had to do. I have been writing since I learned how as a child – recording my feelings and experiences as a young person, with so many bits since then getting discarded. The articles and booklets I published were non-fictional. Poems and short stories got lost as I moved around. The book remained an idea for many years until last year, when my young adult son was struggling with his own decisions, and I felt that I must also lead by example as I struggled through a major change in my own life. A deadline to finish my first book was set.

I acknowledge my son for helping me to commit to finishing this book. I also acknowledge the support and inspiration of other family members who quietly seemed to believe I could do it, even when I did not. I acknowledge my English teachers from my earliest years who helped me to develop my passion for reading and writing and my commitment to this genre of communication. My faith in God and what I was meant to achieve in this life is my ultimate driving force, and I am grateful. It is exciting to have a publisher willing to be on this journey with me.

Chapter One

Ama stood shrouded in the haze of grief that emanated from those around her. It was a day that many would say reflected the solemnity of the occasion. There was no sign of the sun, hidden behind the spread of grey clouds across the wide expanse of sky visible across the grassy plains. There was a momentary silence, a break in the words from the priest who had been speaking for the first ten minutes of the ceremony.

Umbrellas that had been out for most of that time now hung loosely, dripping at the sides of the people gathered around the mahogany casket, which was about to be lowered to the open hole in the ground. A small crowd had gathered to pay their last respects to the man they knew and to the family to whom he had been a much-loved member. In the space filled only with hushed whispers, Ama vaguely hoped that they had had the last of the rain as her feet felt nearly soaked through the closed up black shoes and stockings she wore for the occasion. The hem of her dress weighed against her skin at the top of her calves, and she could think only of ridding herself of these trimmings for a pair of slacks and slippers. But she knew that would not happen anytime soon.

Ama was now the widow, left to mourn the death of a man who had been her husband for closer to three decades, but she felt apart from this group of well-wishers – some family, some friends, some neighbours. She felt separate from those who felt they knew her as much as they had known the husband – the father and hardworking member of their community. Family gathered included their two married children, three grandchildren, one younger brother who was still at university, a few cousins and their families. Theirs had not been a large family of relatives but it was supplemented by members of the community they had called home for most of their lives, including the twenty-nine years in which they were married.

Evans had lived the life he wanted – one of security and stability – and had not fought very hard against the impact of the ailment that had quickly taken over his ability to move around. He had spent the last two years of his sixty-one years being pushed around in a wheelchair, unable to pursue the work that he loved and that was the only source of fulfilment since his early retirement five years previously. The community will miss this stalwart, the man for whom nothing too much could be asked. He had been welcomed into the homes of most of these people because of the commitment he showed to the development of their close-knit community.

Evans' parents had moved into the area when he was just three years old, purchasing the house that had been passed down to Evans after their death. Evans' brother, Todd just two years younger, did not engender the respect that all had for his older brother. He showed no concern, enjoying the activities that Evans had dismissed as frivolous with the allowance that he received.

Ama almost jumped when her granddaughter touched her arm. "Nana, I need to use the bathroom," she announced in a loud whisper above the scraping sound the coffin made against the rocks as it was lowered six feet to the earth below. Ama dragged her thoughts back to the present, "What did you say, Sweetheart?"

"I need to use the bathroom, Nana," her four-year-old granddaughter repeated.

Ama turned to her daughter standing on the other side next to her husband of five years, holding the newest member of their family in her arms with tears rolling down her face, in the throes of sadness at the loss of her father. She quickly turned to her granddaughter, taking her hand quickly, but trying to let the time pass until he reached the bottom. She knew she should be there for these final moments and tried to soothe her oldest grandchild, encouraging her to wait.

"Dust to dust, ashes to ashes..." The voice of the priest reached her again as he said the final prayer for her husband. Then it was time for each member of the family to shovel in some of the soil before the gravediggers took over.

Ama led the mourners in resting the first wreath of flowers on the covered hole in the ground. She felt suddenly overcome by a flood of sadness, saying goodbye to the man who had been a caring companion for all her adult life. She walked with her granddaughter at her side, holding one of her hands as she held the flowers in the other.

"Nana…" The call from Krystal this time was a small, whiny sound, barely audible but enough for her grandmother to hear the urgency. Ama walked away with her quickly towards the washrooms that were not far across the field of tombs.

"Okay, sweetheart, let us go now."

Cars lined both sides of the now narrow street before and after the house that had been home for so many years. There was little room for ongoing traffic, but this was not going to be a problem as neighbours made allowances for the occasion.

Ama was assisted out of the front seat of the car driven by her twenty-eight-year-old son. His wife and only child sat in the back with Krystal, who was very attached to her grandmother.

Ama took her hand, walking to the gate with her older son and his family. She did not relish the long evening that was ahead and wished it was over. These people expected too much from her, and though she also loved her husband, she considered some of their expectations more than a bit unrealistic.

Ama had had her own career and always thought the home was the responsibility of husband and wife. She had always rejected the idea of being a housewife with all that this demanded. She had worked full-time, going back to school when their children had been independent and occupied with their own activities. In that time, she had finally completed a first degree to supplement her professional teaching qualification and later a postgraduate qualification that put her on a different path for a new career.

Ama was eleven years younger than her husband and had been looking forward to a change of career when Evans got sick. She had not thought twice about discontinuing her studies to ensure that he had the best care. She would have expected the same from him if it had been the other way around. They had been partners, and she thought that he had understood and accepted this.

They had raised their children together, with Evans accepting the demands that his wife had made. He had worked hard to be the man she expected, and although he might have fallen short in terms of his very pragmatic disposition, she knew he loved her as she had loved him. She was going to miss him and was not sure how she would manage the loss, but she was not overcome by grief. She knew she would be okay with whatever she chose to do with the rest of her life

"Mummy!"

It was her daughter, calling out to her from across the room. "Mummy, could you help me find…"

Ama had been moving around the room full of their guests as the caterers hired for the occasion served the meal they had picked for the occasion. She received expressions of condolence, hugs and/or looks of sympathy from the people filling the living room and flowing onto the porch and front lawn of the sprawling four-bed/two-bathroom house that Evans' father had built and that they had renovated more than once over the years.

"Yes, Susan?" Ama's response was distracted as she

pulled herself out of the haze of memories.

"Mummy, I'm looking for the pictures we took with you and Daddy five years ago, the last family holiday before…"

Ama reached her daughter, embracing her fragile frame and feeling Susan's tight grip around her body. Susan and her father had shared a special relationship that stretched a little further than the more typical father-daughter connection. As his only daughter, Evans had been particularly protective of his second child, and while she had rebelled when it suited her, she had enjoyed the adoration her father lavished as the protectiveness was gradually enveloped in admiration for the woman she had become.

She had continued to be his little girl, often overshadowing the second son who had come five years later. A connection had developed between them in a way that his wife did not quite understand. Ama had looked on and been happy for her daughter to have such positive attention from the first man in her life. She had known that it would set the standard for her choices of mate in the latter years.

Susan was, in so many ways, a combination of both her parents – the purposeful, driven yet warm, and reflective personality of her mother blended with the quietly laid-back generosity of her father to all and sundry. That generosity was second nature – not considered with any depth of purpose, just who Evans had been. It had been like an armour protecting him from life's harshness. He had revelled in the esteem in which others held him and in return found it easy to be there for them, to provide a net before it was needed, to contribute to the structure of a community that worked tirelessly to manage–representing them where needed to obtain physical resources.

Susan seemed to push her father in a way that Ama had not been able to for most of their marriage, something Ama had accepted from her own childhood experience with her father. In a way, Susan had taken over from the initial challenge that her mother had been to the man who would become her husband in a few short months. Ama had teased and challenged Evans since their meeting, but with the reality of life's demands fuelled by his wife's passion to pursue dreams and seek to create change where she thought it was needed, he had grown less and less enchanted by this aspect of their relationship. He had decided early in their marriage that he was good enough and wanted to be nothing more than the man he was capable of being to his family.

Ama held on to her daughter and allowed her to shed more tears quietly. Together, they walked to the parents' bedroom where Ama found the pictures in a case on a bottom shelf in the wide built-in closet that she had shared with Evans.

"Here they are!"

"Thanks, Mummy. I was telling Cousin Marcus and his family about that holiday and wanted to show them that picture of Daddy with all of us romping on the beach. He had seen so healthy and happy then…"

Mother and daughter filed through the small stack of photographs from that seven-day trip that they had managed to take not so long ago. Jonathan had been home then finishing college, and Ama had insisted that she had needed a break and that the family had not enjoyed time together for a long time – not since the two older ones had been married.

About seven years before that, Andrew had left home to study law, choosing to live closer to the university while working part-time to support himself. Susan had followed next, to go to study medicine just a year later, so the previous holiday had been a goodbye to the two children. The next time they had been together was for weddings. Ama had recognised that with Jon going off in the next two or three years, she and Evans would be alone for the first time in almost as many years as their marriage.

Susan had gotten married the year after finishing her medical degree, on her return home for her internship, to the man she had known since they were both college students.

Andrew had gotten married only a year before that holiday. On that holiday, there were no grandchildren yet. Ama looked over her daughter's shoulder at the photos, seeing her deceased husband looking perhaps a bit overweight but still healthy as he laughed at the young people – his children and their spouses – frolicking on the sunlit beach at the island resort. Ama lounged next to him and seemed also relaxed and pleased to be with her family.

"Yes, he does look well. He looks happy too," she spoke reflectively, remembering that he had not seen him so comfortable since that holiday.

"Marcus and the cousins will be happy seeing him.

They had not seen him for a long time," she spoke as she and her mother left the room and walked back to their guests.

Many of the people gathered for the dinner had left quietly, leaving mostly close family members who sat in small groups, lingering with long moments of silence, as people are wont to do in mourning a loss. Some looked up at Ama as she walked slowly by, casting glances of condolence or just observing how she was managing the loss of the man she had married so long ago. *What will she be doing now?* She got the sense – maybe from the intent looks – that many of them were focused on this. She was still young... she was attractive and elegant to look at. How was she really feeling?

Ama approached some of them and spoke briefly. She did not want to linger at any one table. She did not feel very comfortable with the speculation that filled some of their glances, words unspoken. She spoke quietly and managed to conjure up a smile for everyone. Both Evans and she had lost their parents during the last decade and only had siblings between them. had cousins from his mother's side and they were all present with their families. Todd seemed to have settled down with a wife and now two children and they were all there as was Ama's younger sister who was there with her husband and three children. Her older sister lived abroad and could not make it home in time for the funeral but had sent her love and condolences.

Ama's sisters had always respected Evans, even though he did not inspire much in terms of enthusiasm from them. They thought he was a good man and treated him well. Jon too was in the middle of examinations, and they had thought that it did not make sense for him to miss these. He had seen his father a year previously when he had become seriously ill.

Ama eventually sat down with her one friend she had known from school. Jennie had come alone sitting with a couple of the cousins who were chatting with her. She came closer to Ama as the latter approached and they both headed for a seat in the garden.

"How are you feeling?" Jennie spoke, wanting to console her friend and wanting to understand how she really felt.

"I have never really imagined this day. Maybe it has come sooner than either Evans or I thought it could. I do not really know how I feel, to tell you the truth."

"That's normal, I think," Jennie said after a few seconds. "People often speak of feeling numb after the death of someone close. It may not sink in until after all the rituals are over and everyone has gone back to their lives."

"I suppose so… at least I know I will have to face it."

"I am here for you… whenever you need to talk," Jennie announced, stretching out her hand to hold Ama's, folded on her lap.

"I know…" Ama felt herself smile. She knew that Jennie would be there for her. Her friend who had never married and had been a good friend throughout the years. God-mother to her first child and confidant in the more challenging days of her marriage to Evans.

She knew Jennie was someone she could depend on whenever needed.

Chapter Two

Ama opened her eyes suddenly to the coolness of the evening air. She wondered if she had fallen asleep, submerged as she had been in her reverie – her reverie of an alternative ending to more than a quarter century of marriage… an ending in which she would not be so much the villainess in her own story.

She really did not wish Evans had died. She could not be such an awful person. She would have mourned his death, if not just for herself, then certainly for their family. And they would be a family – in good times and in bad… maybe even more so without the commitment to marriage between them.

Ama gathered her things quickly, not wanting the darkness to descend before she had gotten into her car. This was a somewhat isolated part of the beach she had frequented from childhood, mostly with her own father, but also with family and neighbourhood friends on different outings. It was a bit different now, but she had hoped to find solace in a place that had been joyful in her memory – a time in her life when things were simple, uncomplicated, and innocent.

Ama took a final look at the open sea, with the sun descending into the horizon. How often had she floated on the waters, looking into the sky and dreaming of a dazzling future for herself? She wondered if that dream would ever be realised, even in a small way. The years of marriage and family life had not been in that future, and living it had not allowed her to fulfil those dreams.

Ama had been so young when she married and began a family, without any real thought of what she would have been giving up – travel, adventure, the realisation of dreams. Her father had been willing to invest in her future, studying abroad where she could develop her foreign language skills. Her mother had told her this sometime after she was married and having her first child. Less than a year after her wedding, in the throes of morning sickness, she realised she had become an adult, soon to be a mother. She had been ready to embrace motherhood as she had done marriage – before she could even finish university.

Ama had given up all thought about those plans to attend university abroad, learn a foreign culture and improve in the language to which she had been exposed in high school and college. Those were dreams, along with so many others, not to be realised. She had always had a passion for the well-being of children, but she had thought then it would likely involve caring for other people's rather than her own. Her own would be linked to finding the man of her dreams, but life had brought a different path.

It was now time to go back to reality – the reality in which she had left her husband and made the decision to get a divorce from him. She had expected him to agree, but he had made it clear that it was her idea. It was she who had disappointed so many. Her children were not happy with her. She was alone. Was there a friend who would draw near now? Was there a friend who would understand the dilemma of her new state, her decision to sever all that she had known for a life that was only in her dream, a figment of her imagination or, at best, her idealism?

Ama climbed the steep flight of steps from the coastline to the paved parkway. Hers was one of two cars remaining there. She walked briskly, feeling the chill evening air against her bare arms. The sun had descended quickly in the time she had taken to climb the steep path from the beach. Digging into the bag she carried on her arm, Ama found her keys, opened her car, and got in hastily to ensure she was not the last to leave the compound. The dusk was quiet, in sharp contrast to just an hour or so before when the chatter of families, the shout of children, and the chirping of birds settling among the trees had filled the air.

Ama drove at some speed along the tree-lined road onto the main motorway, turning off after a couple miles to drive a short distance into the compound of the modern high-rise building that included the rented accommodations that were currently her home. There was really no reason to hurry, though. There was no one at home waiting for her. She nonetheless looked forward to being in the safe haven of the apartment that she had recently decorated – the first place she could call home as a single adult.

This was a completely new experience for Ama. She had begun a new and unexpected journey, and there were moments, even now, of sheer terror alternating with moments of absolute joy when she thought that she was now free to pursue the life that she had long ago left behind as part of her youthful dreams. Ama smiled for one moment of glee at the idea as she parked in her spot on the compound. Most of her neighbours seemed to be out, which was not unexpected on a Saturday evening.

Ama drew out the key to her flat, and in a minute was walking through the ground floor of her open-plan living area and through the back door to a small garden and sitting area. This was her favourite spot where she had a view of the forested mountain beyond the area just outside the fence. A low-flowing stream separated her building from a few houses at the bottom of the slope. She had a view of tall trees and sky, taking up some reflection of the sun sinking from the west at the other side of the building. To the right, there was only a short span of the ocean, soon to be invisible in the absence of the sun.

Ama put on a light in readiness for the darkness as she prepared a meal for herself. She was getting very good at this with supermarket purchases that matched her mood as much as her tastes. She tried to maintain a good balance with her choice of wholesome but less common produce. Ama was now using recipes from books she had kept but never used, having mostly prepared dishes that reflected her children's taste. She had continued this long after they started leaving the nest, stuck in the rut that had been her life for too long.

Ama thought about having her meal in front of the television but chose instead to sit at the kitchen counter facing the open door. She would eat and then sit outside for a while with a glass of her favourite rose, another recently embraced idea.

Less than thirty minutes later, Ama was sitting there. It was good to be doing nothing but relaxing. Ama purposefully shifted her thoughts away from the present, her mind drifting to days when she had dared to dream – entertaining thoughts that flickered through her mind, dreams competing with reality.

***

Ama walked along the path, searching for the place to stop. She had not worked out exactly what she was looking for, but was sure she would know the place when she saw it. Once she had found it, she would contact the others. She expected that they would want to join her… well… maybe. She imagined the discussion or the series of outbursts. They were all strong characters – her children, mostly. Her husband would have his moments, but less predictable. In any case, he was likely to wait and see what the place looks like and how strongly she felt about it.

She thought then about what finding this spot would mean. She knew it was more than a temporary camping site, but how much it would define her, she was yet to find out.

Ama had been a child when she first began to feel that she might not be like everyone else. She was not sure about her place in the family. Did everyone have this sense of aloneness, of not knowing for certain the connection to siblings and her parents? The sense of being someone looking in rather than belonging, the tendency to question way beyond the stage where it was cute? They would now call it confrontational or argumentative. But Ama hoped that she was not any of those things. She preferred to think of herself as gentle and sometimes restless of spirit, seeking to know, to find the existence that would explain her knowledge, her awareness, and provide her with that elusive sense of belonging. As usual, her reflections led her to become lost in another era, being still a child with longing to escape to… anywhere!

"Ama! Ama! Where are you?" Ama could hear the irritation and frustration in her mother's voice. She would not be happy finding her younger daughter with one of her novels – or worst yet, daydreaming instead of doing the chores that she had assigned her. They were preparing for her eldest child's big party the next day, and Ama was supposed to help decorate the family living room and patio. But her sister did not really want Ama's help. Every idea she had offered was dismissed, almost as though she had not spoken. Besides, she did not care about things like that anyway.

"Yes, Mother! I'm here… coming!" Ama answered quickly before her mother could find her. She did not know how long she had been sitting in her favourite spot beside the mango tree. It was a nice, shady spot, and from there, she had some seclusion but also a good view of the horizon. It was her place to imagine.

Now, though, she was up from her perch and around the back of the house where she encountered her mother. Easily excitable, her mother lived for those opportunities to entertain, dressing up everything and everyone, and most of all for cooking, using recipes she had found to create those special dishes that most people seemed to enjoy.

"Here I am, Mother!" Ama spoke with a smile in her tone – better to be soothing to her mother. "Do you want me to wash up some wares?"

Ama's mother did not much appreciate help with cooking, and that was fine with her fifteen-year-old daughter, who really hated it anyway... but she was efficient with tidying.

"No, Ama! Your father promised he would buy raisins. I specifically had it on the list I gave him, and still no raisins! I definitely cannot prepare the rice I am preparing without it."

Ama had a good experience of how much these things meant to her mother. The next step would even be tears.

"Don't worry, Mother. I'll get the cash from Daddy and go get the raisins."

Daydreaming had left Ama unaware of the distance she had covered on this life-changing search for home until she realised that she had arrived. She had reached the place she sought. Ama stood transfixed as she gazed at the scene around her. The wide expanse of green seemed to merge with the blueness of the sky and the water falling in a rippling stream to the river below. It was the scene she had held in her imagination, seeing herself now as in a dream, unable to move from where she stood, unbelieving, ecstatic, her heart pounding with excitement and awe at the vision she beheld. She was here! She was here! The excitement built to the point that she could not contain it. She burst out in the most joyful laughter and jumped up and down, spinning around, her knapsack discarded on the grassy plain.

The children arrived one at a time, standing there looking at their mother, a smile growing on each of their faces as they gazed at her – unsure what to make of her now but recognising the joy that could only be infectious. They each dropped their bags, their faces too transformed as they joined her. It was thus that her husband found them. He stood there, arms folded across his chest, watching and shaking his head. This was the woman he had married, the mother of his children, the woman he found it so difficult to keep up with, but the one he would trust – he had trusted – with his life. He could not take his eyes off her. He had not seen this Ama for quite some time but here she was – the woman he loved.

It was at that moment that Ama also looked across at him. They both knew and responded to the communication between them that, thankfully, had not died within the turbulence and the drought of the last few years. They were still here. Thank God. And they both ran, catching up to each other with a gleeful shout of pure joy as their children stopped and looked – the brief moment in which their parents hugged each other – a brief moment before they joined in, dropping finally to the grassy plain for the rest they needed. They were here!

When did Ama first dream of this place – the special place to which she would escape? Escaping was something she had always done. Having a discontent with the present, she created her own from as far back as she could remember. As a child looking for a place beyond her reality, she daydreamed during a class that did not offer as much as she wanted or during an interaction with the friends she had made. Daydreaming as she escaped to her room after a disagreement with her mother. Escaping came easily too in the novels she read, painting a picture of life in places beyond her shores where other children in far-off countries lived in interesting places and enjoyed adventures that were sharply in contrast to the mundane experience of her village. She had thought then that there was more out there and the wonder of finding it and living there consumed her dreams and maybe her attitude to life. Escaping in her books grew with her in the historical dramas and romance into imagined places worlds away. She travelled the world that was vibrant and awe-inspiring, so real it became part of her and her experiences.

Finding the quiet place where she could recuperate from her discontent, worry, and sadness of not belonging became just as important. Mountains and plain, green trees and endless expanses of grassy plains, the river, the lake, the ocean stretching off into the horizon – her special place, not contaminated by the world, serene and naturally beautiful, where she could shed her tears and equally laugh without any other reason than the joy of being able to – for those moments, fully alive and free. It was the place where she could imagine people sharing their humanity with one another and becoming all that they could be. And it may have contributed to her fearlessness in pursuing things that others dismissed as unattainable. What else could she do?

Finding what really matters is the only compensation she could have for being forced to live a life that often seemed shallow and too routine to really matter. Are the things so many people have come to believe the truth, or are they powerful, well-developed ideas thrust upon the multitude? Was anything consistent, or do people just speak out what is convenient at the time? What are the universal concepts that must define our attitudes and values? Is it Justice and Equality, Rights and Freedom? Or is it Power and Oppression? Religions speak of love and then practiced inequality and division that inspire conflict and hate. Politicians, Economists, Psychologists… whose side do they take in this relentless quest for the resources of this world we inhabit? To not judge means we must be striving towards the perfection that must be our birthright, our reason for being.

Chapter Three

Ama rushed through her chores, anxious to get it done so she could join her friends on the back porch. Their father did not encourage their interaction with other children in the neighbourhood. He forbade any visits to other people's houses to play, and the children who visited Ama and Shelley usually ran off when he arrived home after work. But their mother turned a blind eye to these gatherings, as she was engaged in her own ideas of perfection within her house. In their father's absence, everyone was freer to do the things that made them happy.

Ama was looking forward to leading the small group of children who would gather to 'play school', the imaginative play in which she was always the teacher. In her enthusiasm, she had suffered quite a few mishaps, e.g. a deep cut on her leg from using one of her father's razors to sharpen a pencil. On another occasion, she had organized a field trip to the mountains. She had made sure to have all the food, water, and other equipment to spend the day hiking and having a picnic in an idyllic area of the hillside laden with trees and fruits of the tropical forest. She knew the trail from outings with her father, going to clear some ground and plant a few popular crops e.g. corn and peas.

Ama had had no idea of the time and a couple of hours

seemed like a day when they returned before midday.

Ama woke up looking forward to the first day of school. The holidays had been full of the usual activities, usually not far from home. Eight weeks at home was a lot of time for her to indulge her imagination. Hustling through chores around house cleaning, Ama had had long hours to go through the bookshelves. She had read almost every book there – mostly fiction, from different genres and different eras – usually when she felt bored and had nothing else to do. Long hours were filled with activities she had created. It was the time before cable television and other expansions in social media, and she was good at entertaining herself. Forget about the little accidents that her mother did not relay to her father.

Ama has always been good at going beyond the boundaries. From her earliest years, she had stood up to her grandmother, who may have seen herself as the matriarch, standing over her daughter and son-in-law, Ama's father, even while enjoying his hospitality – days spent in the home he was creating for his wife and children. She did not like Ama's boldness. "Take your eyes out of mine," she would say when Ama sat around listening to 'adult conversations', soaking in the words, ideas, and values being expressed. Children were supposed to know their place, and she thought the Ama operated outside of those rules. She had never been gentle with her second granddaughter and had contributed to Ama growing up feeling overlooked and irrelevant.

Ama's grandmother, called 'Mama' by everybody who knew her – including her daughter – doted on her first granddaughter, seeming to have little left to embrace anyone else with the same enthusiasm. Ama realised early that she could never please her, so she did not see the point of even trying. Ama could recall her fingers being knocked with the hair comb as she tried to find out how Mama was combing her hair, sitting on the floor between her legs. Her voice and manner had seemed unnecessarily sharp when she reprimanded her not to touch. Even without Mama present in the household, the relationship between her mother and her older daughter was a tight one from which Ama was excluded. It was nonetheless not well-received when she gravitated towards her father whenever he was around.

Ama's close relationship with her father did not mean that she was willing to accept his rulebook in all its entirety. At eight, nine, ten years, she could not accept that girls must not climb trees. What was the reason for this rule? For Ama, no logical response meant no good reason. The proliferation of trees laden with fruit, especially mangoes, invited her, with branches that reached down low enough for her to access with some help from a step ladder. Sitting high up on a sturdy branch was the nearest she could get to the treehouses enjoyed by children far away who had great adventures. She had a view of the hillsides, mostly green but increasingly dotted with wooden and then concrete structures. She had a view of the ocean with intermittent glimpses of a moving shape – ships going places she longed to visit.

As a pupil at the local primary school, Ama looked forward to the learning and some friendships that she had developed, but it was mostly about doing something that had to be done. Education was not questioned in Ama's family. Education meant upward mobility – being able as an adult to have more and do more than her parents could. Having an education meant getting a profession that allowed her to make her own decisions about the life she wanted. Education was knowledge, but even more, it was a means to an end. Ama learned that at an early stage, sitting at her father's knee, following him around, and listening to his stories. Her determination was unquestionable. From this age, she was aware of a relentless personal quest – for truth, for justice, for adventure, and to follow her own destiny.

Ama had two more years at primary school, and she looked forward to the next step. The last two weeks of the vacation had been spent packing and unpacking her new school bag. This followed the annual day out shopping with her parents. Although she often went out with her mother, this day out with her father was the highlight of her year. Shopping for books and other school equipment was followed by lunch, when she got to explore tastes that she did not have much chance to indulge. Her father was good with this ritual, choosing nice places to eat, and she knew he enjoyed having these special times as much as she did. The money spent did not seem to be an issue either, as it would have been with her mother.

Back home, Ama enjoyed the idea of having all her books and other new things for school. Books were covered with brown paper and labelled, helped by her mother, who had beautiful handwriting. Everything was there to ensure that she was ready for school, ready to do her best and achieve good results. This was as much as her parents could do – making sure that she was never absent, following the rules, respecting the teachers, and generally not getting into trouble.

Clothes were laid out for Ama and her sister, and they got ready, bags in hand, as they began the long walk to school. It was a familiar route, and they had the company of most other children in the neighbourhood. The first day was always exciting – meeting the new teacher and finding out where you would sit. Most other things were not new, as the building doubled as the place of worship each Sunday.

"Ama! Ama!" She looked around as she turned to corner to the school compound, seeing the round figure of another girl hurling towards her. She recognized her classmate, Brigitte. A year older, Brigitte was an early developer and tended to be loud and a bit aggressive in her relationship with other children. She was often in some form of conflict with someone, younger or older than herself, over some trivial matter – usually because someone either said something about her or rejected her attempts to be included in a game. Brigitte had decided that Ama was not like the other children and had therefore decided they were friends.

Ama lingered a few moments to allow Brigitte to catch up. Even before Brigitte reached her side, Ama had a whiff of a musty and stale scent that accompanied her.

Looking closely at the girl, Ama wondered – not for the first time – how Brigitte managed to be sweaty and dishevelled so early in the morning and even on this, the first day of the new school year. Ama wondered if she could do or say something to help Brigitte with this. She would be ten years soon and knew that Brigitte had repeated their last year and was a bit older than most of them. How was it that she could not take care to be clean and neat on the first day of school?

Ama knew some people did not have as much as her family did, but her father had always said they were not rich. Her mother did not do paid work and instead made everything for them. Meals were regular and always well done, as was the sewing of everything they wore beside shoes. They did not have fancy things like some of the other children she knew, but her father always insisted that clothing just needed to be clean and without holes. Rips in clothing were regularly managed and mended when necessary. She had never been to Brigitte's house and did not know her family.

"Hi, Brigitte!" Ama smiled, looking closely at her classmate.

"Hi, Ama... you reached school... same time as me..." Ama was breathless, making heaving sounds as she adjusted the bag on her shoulder.

Ama knew that Brigitte lived in the area around the school, certainly much closer than she did, although she was usually late, walking in after the morning assembly in the courtyard. Ama's father always insisted on their being punctual, and first day was also a special time for her, which meant she woke earlier than usual. Brigitte, it seemed, felt that same excitement to be on time.

The noise as they entered the school confirmed that they were not the only ones anxious to be early for the first day. Who is the teacher? Will he or she be strict? The crowd of children grew as the time passed, with children talking to one another about some of their activities over the two months away from school but also showing off the new things they had acquired. Soon the bell was heard above the shouts and chatter, and the children moved quickly into their lines just as the teachers appeared from the school building. The children stood as they had done the previous year, waiting for the announcements. They were eager to hear about their classes for the new school year.

***

Ama drifted through the primary school years, never achieving the level of recognition that even then she may have sought. A bright pupil who teachers identified as somewhat above average, able enough to be skipped over the second year of Infants to the first primary class, but still never good enough, never in front or centre-stage. A nondescript child who was gradually noted to be outspoken but not worthy of attention. Ama was one year away from the exam to qualify for a secondary school when she learnt that teachers may be affected by issues other than a child's ability. Even in the classroom, family status and physical appearance, including skin colour, were issues that impacted on a teacher's judgement.

The second disappointment came when Ama was not

able to move to the next class, where she would be allowed to sit the exam. Having skipped a year, she was now too young to sit the secondary school attainment test with the rest of her class. This led to Ama's mother's unexpected decision to get her to a more prestigious school where she hoped Ama would have a better chance for her ability to be recognised. She implored Ama's father to break his rule of not using his access to persons in higher places to obtain favours for his family. Ama did obtain that transfer to a new school in the city but still without the benefit of the skipped year.

Secondary school was one of the most eventful and meaningful periods of Ama's life. School life offered an array of opportunities for her to discover different ways of living. Classmates from different backgrounds became friends as they moved through school together. Ama's popularity was based on a combination of her academic ability, diligence in adhering to the main rules relating to her physical care and adherence to the standards of the school – punctuality, regularity, good organization – and her confidence in standing up for herself and her peers on issues that affected their day-to-day life at school. Ama was able to question the rules that seemed unnecessary and unequally distributed, especially those that were coined by individual teachers. She did this with clarity and with enough respect that reduced any likelihood of complaints, with no negative consequences to be addressed either by Ama's parents or the school authority.

After an encounter with Ama, teachers usually did not complain, accepting that she managed to achieve their respect with her candour and determination. Her achievement was honoured with opportunities to participate in events to develop her leadership qualities and for her to have experiences that would not be normally accessible to a child that was not from an affluent background. Ama had parents whose best qualities were in their interest, if not educational skills, to pursue the best for their children. Ama enjoyed the opportunities she was given, including weekends away from home for fun combined with learning and a range of extra-curricular activities.

Even so, Ama felt the limitations being imposed by some, like her middle school teacher who insisted that she was 'academically gifted' and therefore 'not musically gifted', refusing to allow her the opportunity to be included in the group of girls chosen for learning how to play her country's national instrument, which turned out to be the only one developed in the twentieth century.

No individual best friends but a friend to most was Ama's path that served her well for most of those years. She never suffered from lack of opportunities to visit and be visited by friends at home. Birthday celebrations were always fun, and Ama's mother, in particular, enjoyed when she had friends over, especially with the diversity obvious in the group.

In the midst of this, Ama had another life. A life in which she shared little of her inner self. A mentor she met in the latter years counselled her about her fear of letting others see her as she really was. Ama felt years older than her peers and did not feel that they could ever understand the thoughts, the person that she kept hidden from them. She dealt with mundane as well as serious issues, but her deepest reflections on the meaning of life could not be shared. She enjoyed having that personal space in which there was time for sadness, disappointment and wonder about the universe. Ama realised that even while she laughed at the teenage antics of her friends, she in actuality, laughed at the foolishness of it all, at how idle and meaningless it all was. She felt she had a wisdom that was beyond her years that did not give her comfort. It made her feel alone, even in a group, and challenged her to pursue the truth that seemed to lie beyond her reach.

Ama contemplated possibilities for the years ahead but, in actuality, could not see herself in those years. There seemed to be nothing but the present. Ama lacked for nothing material, none that was necessary, but felt a void for everything that seemed to occupy the minds of those around. She questioned the existence of her parents and what she meant to people in her family. She felt overlooked and unimportant, someone who did not matter. She consumed books about people in far-off times and locations, finding more in common with the stories told about them. She questioned the real purpose of her existence despite working on the obvious achievements that were expected. She did what was expected to keep up with school, nothing more, and had to accept when her school head recognised that she could do better, always with the sixth sense that Ama had more than she was giving. Ama knew she needed more for her to invest more.

With secondary school behind her at the end of her

teenage years, Ama faced the world of work, starting university a year later and struggling to find purpose in the course of work. At one stage, she believed that she had found the truth, choosing more religious pursuits and began the adult years married to a man who she had known for a few short months. Getting on with it, Ama also entered the only profession she had ever considered.

Chapter Four

Your best is good enough – the theme developed as Ama sought to impact the lives of the students she met in her first real job as an assistant teacher. There were those who had stood out with a reverse effect that she would not be able to dismiss in the years ahead.

Jimmy was in the last year of his primary education. It was a time when most of his classmates seemed to embrace the demands while they looked forward excitedly to the next year and being in secondary school. Jimmy did not understand what that excitement was about. He felt scared about the whole idea of greater demands being made on him. He remembered the days when he was happy coming to school and meeting his friends. There had been so much to talk about and so much time to do so. Without any brothers or sisters at home, school was the place to enjoy games with his friends. The time in the classroom seemed to be worth all of this. They had to be quiet, to listen, and learn to do different things, but it had all seemed new and interesting.

Jimmy would not have said that he now hated to come to school, but the signs suggested that he was not far off.

"Jimmy! Jimmy, pass your book!"

Jimmy was jerked out of his dream and at once noted that

he had not completed the Maths exercise. Another breaktime to be spent indoors, rather than outside with his friends.

The walls of the classroom seemed to close in around him as the rest of the class streamed through the open doors to the playground. Nobody bothered to call him or check to find out if he was coming. They had become used to Jimmy staying indoors. He was not keeping up with the amount of work they had to finish each day, and the teacher was determined that every pupil needed to do this. Jimmy seemed unusually sad these days as well and tired, always resting his head on the desk. His close friends had tried giving him a nudge from time to time but had now given up. Too many times each day, the teacher called on Jimmy to sit up, to pay attention, and to finish the exercises the students were given.

Jimmy often did not complete homework, saying that he did not understand or that he did not get a chance to do it. Years later, Ama still remembered Jimmy and other students who had struggled in the classroom. In the small community where they lived, everyone either knew each other or knew someone who did. From their time in primary school, Ama had learned a bit about Jimmy's family, about their alcoholic father and the untimely death of their mother from an unknown illness.

Jimmy would have been going through the effects of this tragic situation. There had seemed to be no room for children like him in the classroom or even the school. Ama had been in the habit of listening to adults talking to each other and knew that many would have known about different family circumstances. They had not, however, seen how the rules can change while they were at school. Ama had moved out of the area for secondary school and had never met Jimmy again. She, however, thought about him and the others who had impacted on the choices she had made.

Then there was Kara, whose father had spoken to Ama about her anxiety over the pending Secondary entrance examinations. Kara had physical and behavioural presentations of difficulty coping. She tended to be a quiet and timid child in the classroom, and it had been important to help her to believe that she was able to succeed by doing just the best that she could. The approach taken in the classroom was not only for Kara but for everyone, bringing a general awareness that each child was unique in terms of ability and circumstances, and the teaching would bridge all needs. In the classroom, the children responded to an approach that was inclusive and nurturing rather than competitive and isolating, which was interpreted as detrimental for all in the longer term. The children bought into the belief that your best was good enough, and this became the class motto with resounding success.

Ama was pursuing her first degree when her life changed forever. She did not know it while she walked along the wide-open spaces of the campus, enjoying the level of discussion she found not only in the lecture halls but in the social and political groups that were popular among the budding social scientists. She got involved in the newspaper and made friends among those who offered different views from the people she had known thus far. She spent long evenings on campus, unafraid and ready to explore and enjoy every minute of this new world.

It started first with her attendance on an ordinary day at an event she had planned for weeks. When she met him, he did not seem remarkable in any way. She was introduced to him by a friend, Winnifred (or Winnie), who had only met him that morning while Ama was delayed by a lecture at the university not far from the place where the conference was being held. It was a religious event with a speaker who was a guest of the local parish.

He stayed with them. He seemed to have found the friends he was looking for and remained at their side throughout the lectures. He stayed during the breaks and the late evening events. He stayed until they became a threesome, known to everyone who participated in the weeklong event. He was entertaining and made them laugh. He had a lot to say, constantly introducing ideas that got Ama talking to him as he also shared views that she found new and refreshing – nothing she had found in the young men she had met so far, even at university, where they seemed to have very little to say about life beyond economics or politics. She noticed but had not found it strange that Winnie had drifted away, finding time to go off with other people. Winnie was not much of a talker and could easily have found their discussions a bit too much.

Ama also started to find it helpful to have him around with transport to take them on a few jaunts, and she grew into teasing him relentlessly. One of the subjects was his car, which they often had to give a push to start. A few years older than Ama, she thought it was great to have someone more mature as a friend. His name was Evans, and eventually, she began to wonder what would become of him.

Chapter Five

Very few people knew the story of Ama and Evans during those early years. How they became a couple was not the usual story. They were just becoming friends when the plan shifted to marriage. It was an unexpected event for those who knew them almost as much as for Ama and Evans themselves. A declaration of attraction from Evans one carefree afternoon tumulted them into a declaration of 'happy ever after' – or perhaps 'commitment ever after'.

Ama was not sure how it happened. To understand the course of events, one would need to go back to the time of incredible religious fervour that permeated the thinking of their world at that time. These were communities focused on the renewal of their Christian faith, believing that they were capable of making significant changes to the way people lived. They thought they could move mountains and proceeded to set up those groups of believers who were 'called', drawing inspiration from leaders who must have been waiting for an opportunity just like this one.

At twenty-one, Ama recognised that she had always been a dreamer, and when Evans came along, she thought he was as well. She had not thought beyond friendship when she had thought of Evans, but she had wondered, as they drew closer together in the friendly threesome, if he would indeed end up being more to one of them. Often in the following weeks, it had seemed like just the two of them – Ama and Evans – but this was not acknowledged as anything significant when they continued to meet. She again acknowledged that Winnie, the friend who had brought them together was not one to talk much about anything. She seemed to laugh her way through life, perhaps choosing to ignore the trauma of her own family and instead to engage in a fantasy of her own. In the end, though, Ama and Evans coming together may have interfered with her plans and over the years, it became obvious that she had not forgiven them or mostly Ama, for going off and getting married, with all the implications for the community life they had planned. As it turned out, Winnie had not been the only one.

But before all of that unravelled, there was Ama and Evans talking more when the opportunity arose.

Still all together, youth group meetings led to fun trips to the cinema before expanding into the two of them going further afield to beaches and long drives to faraway places that Ama had never thought of visiting. Their friendship was based on adventure. It was fun going out and getting to know the countryside that Ama had not travelled through before.

Without a family car, her father had not undertaken much in terms of family outings beyond the boundaries of the city. A few months passed with periods of no interaction, which picked up when Ama took on a vacation job not far from where Evans had worked since leaving primary school.

Evans was partly a self-taught individual talking

about reading self-help books and lessons he had learned about healthy eating and issues surrounding success in life. There were no real signs of these being implemented, but his confidence in expressing his ideas and theories resounded with some of what Ama expressed from her limited life experiences, which were mostly dreams. Evans was also involved in a group of young professionals and had managed to become the leader of the religious youth group when they had met. He was not what Ama may have dreamed about in many ways, except that he expressed the ideas one would expect of a man of substance.

Evans had come from what people might identify as humble life, generally content and without sign of purpose linked to achievement of goals and aspirations for themselves and their children. They seemed to live each day as it came, happy and unaware of the demands of the world they lived in or so it seemed. From Ama's early meeting with Evans, he tried to set himself apart from this, never fully sharing the personal bits about himself with the people with whom he interacted in the social circles of the groups to which he belonged. None of these relationships resulted in visits to Evans' home. None of these relationships resulted in personal sharing about his limited formal education, and none of these persons including the teachers among them were allowed to help him in his attempts to make up for the education gaps in those early days.

Ama never realised how much meeting Evans' family had impacted her. She never recovered from fighting to ensure that her life with Evans was nowhere close to the way his family had lived before his siblings each moved away into their new families. Over the years, she had grown to love his mother, a generous person who laughed things away until the death she had predicted would happen at a relatively early age. It became a mission for Ama that in her life with Evans, they would not come anywhere near to accepting the life his mother may have felt forced to live. It was good that Evans had insisted he was different and had a different plan for his life. With her youthful idealism, and perhaps also from the sheltered life that she had lived thus far, Ama had accepted that this was possible without questioning how he planned to achieve it. She believed she could help him to fulfil his dreams.

It was on one of the two-some outings, amid laughter and camaraderie, that Evans expressed his attraction to Ama. She had sensed something different in his mood but had not considered what it was. She did not turn him away, going along with the shift in their relationship that, in short weeks ahead, catapulted into a life time commitment, with both submitting to the force of a different life within a tight community. The people around them, seemingly sharing her aspirations, encouraged them that marriage was the necessary step to prevent this relationship from disrupting the work that had been undertaken.

"Do you know this man? Who is his family?" Ama's father questioned the relationship and his daughter's expressed intention with deep concern, which was dismissed by the overconfident Ama in her youthful naïveté.

"I am not marrying his family, Daddy!" She smiled

believing it to be a point her father should concede. Whether he conceded or not, he could not fight her. She got what she wanted and moved forward, saving him the expense of a second wedding for his daughters in one year. There was to be no expensive reception. The church ceremony would be enough, the new couple had decided.

In the years ahead, Ama had not been able to identify what level of vulnerability had allowed her to respond the way she did to Evans in the weeks after the quasi-proposal. She had managed to convince herself that she had met her soulmate, ignoring all other warnings, spoken and unspoken. Ama had dived fully clothed into the watery depths of that relationship, and before she realised it, she had committed herself to marriage and family.

In just a few months, they were married. No time to waste – there were things to do. Ama did not finish her degree, and she had found something else to occupy her attention. She had not found the course of study she had really wanted, but she saw the opportunity to do something different. Heeding the warnings of those older and wiser was not an option. How is it that the young have such a sense of invincibility?

Seemingly convinced that they know it all, and did not have to entertain the ideas of those who had lived experiences?

It was a year later when Ama awoke to the realisation that she was in a marriage – a state of commitment to a man she barely knew. But there was no turning back. She was going to be a mother, and in the years ahead, one child became three as Ama embraced the choice she had made as a mission – the greatest one, perhaps, of her life, but one she vowed to complete. There was no room for failure with the lives of children at risk. Evans was not the man of her dreams but the man of her reality.

Even in her youth, Ama had not thought she would ever find that one person, not really expecting to find someone who will fit her description of all that was important to her.

Certainly, there had been no hurry. There was still so much to do, and she had not even started. But maybe there had been other plans for her life, and it was in the place that Evans featured. She did not know if the man who would meet her demands ever existed. She accepted that Evans was the compromise that, for some reason still unbeknownst to her, she had needed to make. She accepted Evans at his word – that he could be a good husband and father to their children, that he would be prepared to follow through on what they had agreed as most important: protecting their life together and sharing responsibility for raising their children.

Years later, Ama recognised that Evans may not have known himself that he was never up to the task – well not in the areas that became increasingly important for Ama because they were missing. Ama realised that she was as alone as she ever was as Evans seemed happy to dwell at the surface. Ama began to see him as someone who did not bother with reflection, and that again, she was not being seen. Evans never admitted that he had dropped out a few years on when the demands of their growing family had increased.

Evans saw himself as a good person, a description that he worked to embrace and that was generally undisputed. He was a typical 'nice guy'. Ama remembered her Secondary school principal providing an unusual definition of the word, that was not more than living out one's life along the lines of the most obvious, doing just enough. To Ama, Evans did not make any demands on himself beyond what was normally expected. He found it hard to hold himself to the constant demands of anyone, particularly a wife with ideals and dreams that he could not quite grasp. Not to be admitted, he insisted that what he was able to do was, in all actuality, all that Ama needed, whether she accepted it or not. Evans prided himself on knowing.

And so it was – a marriage that was destined to fail in the world in which there were constant demands. Not prepared to admit to this, Ama held on with dear life for the dream of fulfilment and convinced herself that this was achievable for many years. Until that fateful day. Until that day when she saw what was in front of her and stopped believing. She saw the impossibility of her relationship with Evans. How was she to convince him and those around her of it? She had worked so hard, Evans with her, working to convince everyone that they were a match made in heaven despite the odds that some people noted, despite the odds that may have caused most to wonder. Did they look on, knowing what both Evans and Ama would not accept?

There was no conflict between Evans and Ama when it came to the actual step to end their marriage, and in a shorter time than was expected, the deed was done. It was not long before Ama decided that she could not stay to explain, to try to convince, and to face the derision even of the people closest to them. Instead of trying, she ran. She left it all – the adult children to whom she was only now coming out as a person and the man whom she felt could inspire them to see what he saw. Ama did not belong there and decided to run away from it all. She ran because trying to convince anyone was not something she could do.

Leaving was not difficult, as Evans accepted the arrangements that were made and seemed ready to continue his life almost uninterrupted. Ama had started the process –clearing away and/or storing some items, packing up the few treasures that she wanted to keep as reminders of the best of times or just the keepsakes of hers and her children's history. The children had their lives and would be able to go on with their plans. Jonathan may still need her at times, and they were in constant contact as he finished off his computer engineering degree. They would have time to process what this meant not only for them but for their parents.

Ama's movement out of the home she had shared alone with Evans in the last few years – after their children had moved away – and into the modern apartment complex had given her the much-needed time alone. With months of reflection behind and stretching into the future, she finally knew she needed to get far away. She followed through with her desire to finish off university qualifications, taking the steps that ensured there was no turning back. Finally, she bought a ticket and she got on the flight. Maybe she was running away or just putting a healthy distance between what she had known for most of her life and what was possible in the new life she needed to create for herself.

Ama fled across the Atlantic to a place she had longed to visit so many times before. It was one of the things she had never managed to do in the years of marriage and motherhood. She had subdued all her dreams attached to the single life she had envisaged for herself – all that had occupied her mind and aspirations as a teenaged girl. Why she had not pursued them instead of settling down in the small community, only to be swept away by another kind of dreaming? She had not pursued any of them except having had the good sense to finish her first degree in psychology and other job-related courses, hoping to be qualified at some stage to set up a practice doing something that would also allow her to earn a living on her own terms. As it turned out, that had been enough to disrupt the 'happy ever after' life she and Evans had planned. It had given her a way out – an opportunity to begin again.

Chapter Six

"Welcome aboard," the flight attendant repeated, with her smile in place, ushering the long line of passengers boarding the late evening flight. Ama would not arrive at her destination until the next morning. She did not expect to be met by anyone. The friend she had corresponded with for years was not told of her flight from the only place Ama had ever lived. She did not plan to land on her doorstep unexpectedly. She had booked a place at a Bed and Breakfast, where she would stay for a few days, time to contact her friend before travelling to a more permanent place of abode.

Ama had been accepted into a two-year postgraduate programme in Psychotherapy and secured living accommodations as close as possible to the university campus. Thank God she had not completely abandoned her studies. Pursuing this programme, along with living expenses, had taken most of her savings, including her early retirement money from the job she had held down for most of her marriage but she thought it would be worth it. She would go to school and meet new people, giving her time to get to know a new country. She would make sure that she was happy. She was able to secure a student visa for the duration and would then move to a resident's visa once she found a job. She had worked it all out.

Ama's flight landed at the international airport at nine a.m. the next morning, four hours ahead of the time she had left behind. The flight had been mostly uneventful. Very few families with small children travelled in this direction at this time of year. The weather was a cool eighteen degrees Celsius, and she wore the light jacket she had bought for the trip. Worn over her long-sleeved, high-necked jersey, she felt comfortable with a pair of khaki-coloured slacks and her feet covered in her ankle-high closed-up footwear. Her hair was swept back in a low bun, and she had redone her light make-up in the tiny bathroom after washing her face and brushing her teeth. She was ready to embark on her new life. Independent woman, strong, and capable. She had raised three children. Of course, she had had some help from Evans, but she had been the main person in planning as well as in execution. The children had not done badly. For certain, she could do this now. For her.

When Ama finally got through customs, most passengers were already in the baggage claim area. Lots of suitcases cluttered the area as attendants pulled away those that were not claimed by those present. With her handbag slung over her shoulders, Ama pushed her small suitcase containing her laptop and other items including a change of clothing just in case, finding the baggage claim area to collect the rest of her luggage. Thank God for the ability to follow signs and to be able to ask questions when necessary. Not as confident as she should have been, she had stopped more than one person along the way, but she was where she was supposed to be.

Ama had to collect one larger and one medium-sized suitcase she had used for her latest adventure. Both were gifts from her ex-colleagues. She had heard about people's luggage being misplaced, especially on such long flights, and hoped she would not have that experience.

Scanning the baggage circling around, Ama finally rushed forward, seeing one of her own. She pulled it out and set it aside, not waiting more than another two minutes before her second one appeared. This was a bit heavier, filled with a lot of books and Memorabilia, she remembered. She struggled on her own to pull it out of the carrier and dropped it heavily on the floor before having to lift it onto the trolley she had managed to secure for herself.

Ama checked for her passport and wallet in her bag. She had managed to secure some cash at the bank before leaving home. In her passport, she had a sheet with the address of her accommodations. She was prepared as she made her way along the path for those with nothing to declare but her belongings. She finally reached the wide-open area where family and friends waited, moving ahead of the background of people moving around at different paces, some sitting in preparation for a longer wait.

Ama made the necessary arrangements for a taxi to get her to her destination before pushing her trolley ahead of her. Out in the fresh morning air, with a somewhat dim glow of sunlight, she had her first experience of early autumn. It was a chilly morning as she had imagined, and she was grateful that she had gotten the right advice for attire. Within another thirty minutes, Ama was on her way, having easily identified the taxi when it appeared. She got in quickly as the driver loaded her suitcases into the trunk.

The drive to her guest house was not supposed to be long and maybe not in a populated place at this time of year. They passed a few buses and cars speeding along the wide four-lane motorway, and in fifteen minutes, she had arrived. Relatively near the airport, it was one of a few tall buildings, mostly hotels, separated by larger clusters of greenery.

***

"Ama! Ama!"

Ama looked up from the book she was holding as she squatted on the mat she had spread on the grassy plain in front of the library in the main area of the university campus.

There were lots of young students in groups or pairs, enjoying the sunshine that appeared to be well-appreciated by all. This was the first day since she had completed the registration process, ensuring all fees were paid, course enrolment completed, and that she had the necessary identification card for access to the university facilities. She had made sure that she had a phone plan to get in touch with the only person she knew in this first chapter of her new life.

"Jennie!" Ama's voice was tinged with a gasp of surprise as she saw her old friend just a couple feet away from her. Jennie was all smiles as she ambled along, appearing more than a bit out of place among the throng of jeans-clad fellows poised in different forms of outdoor activity, full of the exuberance of youth. Jennie did not look so well, Ama thought, as she seemed to struggle to move in short strides towards her friend. She had gained quite a few pounds since her last visit home almost ten years ago and clothed in a floral-patterned cotton dress worn with a pair of ankle-high boots. She shaded her face from the glare of sunlight with a hat which momentarily got caught in the breeze, causing Jennie to dash in ungainly fashion to the side trying retrieve it, just as it dropped to the ground.

Ama got quickly to her feet, meeting her good friend halfway and wrapping her arms around her in excitement. It was hard to believe they were both finally together again after all these years exchanging letters. Jennie had invited Ama to visit so many times until she had given up trying to uproot her school chum from the duties of family life. She had always wanted Ama to pull away just enough to enjoy some well-earned fun, if just for a few weeks. Ama had not been able to make that step, devoted to her children and her husband, she had stayed fully focussed on the life she had chosen. Until now.

Jennie and Ama had been good friends from primary school, with both having gone to the same secondary school when Jennie's family had migrated. They had become closer, Ama thought, since Jennie lived abroad, maybe with more to share that was of interest to Ama. Unlike Jennie, Ama had stayed on to finish college, planning to take a year or two off before going to university. Jennie had never been overly academic but the friends had shared an interest in teaching with Jennie choosing to complete teacher training almost immediately, after settling into her new home. She had enjoyed working with primary aged children also making use of the annual vacation periods to indulge her second passion.

Jennie had spent a lot of her vacation time travelling, sending Ama postcards from her more exotic destinations, visiting Ama in the country she had left more than twice in the first twenty years but not recently. In between, she had managed to move into a flat of her own, only to move back in again with her parents when her mother, then her father, had become ill. As the only child of her two parents, there was no one else more able to take care of them. Her aunt and uncle, who lived some distance away from the family home, struggled themselves with the issues that often came with aging. They seem to have been very supportive based on what Jennie had shared with Ama over the last five to ten years but could not take on the responsibility for her parents' care. That had to fall to Jennie.

Both parents had since died within a year of each other, and Jennie had found herself alone. She had come close to marriage a couple of times over the first twenty years she had lived with and then apart from her parents, but the final commitment seemed to have eluded her. She had not spoken of any close relationships for some time, and Ama thought that she may have given up on the idea of finding someone she could settle down with, especially when she had found herself as the main caregiver for her parents.

Ama was finally here visiting her most loyal friend and pulling away from the embrace, they were finally able to give each other a close look. This was the friend she remembered. Up close, she saw the laughter in her eyes as she remembered the friend who was always optimistic and getting them into some situation that she, for one, always found hilarious. They were both laughing now. Jennie also scrutinised her friend very briefly, as she was wont to do, brushing past this to pull her friend towards the picnic area Ama had created. She took the chaise lounge while Ama sat next to her on the mat, ready to catch up with her friend.

There was no need for Ama to go into details of her final separation from Evans. Jennie had been part of the journey, even while being far away. No real explanations were necessary. She was the only person who had information, at least from Ama's point of view. The news was more about how Ama was coping, especially with the impact on the rest of the family and the plan she was crafting for the next few years of her life.

Evans showed the tendency to be somewhat more difficult in later exchanges, leading to Ama's final departure reminiscent of the initial trauma and communication from him could be unexpected and very upsetting for Ama.

Ama was still reeling from the family meeting that they had with the children, Jon via internet from his current place of abode. They were not all able to respond to Ama's initial request for understanding. They were all aware of the differences between their parents though maybe at different levels. The boys, twenty-two and twenty-eight years old were more ready to accept the decision that their mother had made and in the days after had made some attempts to manage their father's initial unwillingness to accept that their mother had good reasons for her decision. Their daughter, the middle child, the apple of her father's eye, seemed to feel personally violated by their mother's decision and seemed to lean to sympathy with her father despite her well-meaning attempts to remain neutral. The relationship continued as they both strove for normalcy, but it was a difficult time for everyone. Ama had difficulty with the shifts in Evans's responses, accepting the decisions made but maybe wanting to control the narrative.

There were times when Ama could empathise with the depth of their disappointment, when she was not overcome by her own pain and need for understanding from children who were after all, adults with family experiences and responsibilities. Surely, they could find common ground. Ama wondered if her daughter was measuring her mother's decision with her own situation as a married woman with two children of her own. She had always seen her husband as like her father in some ways. If that first family meeting was difficult, the weeks later had been painful for Ama as she tried to balance her children's needs with her need to be loved and accepted – not just as their mother but as a person.

Ama had shared some of her feelings with her sister, who had tried to be kind and understanding. This was soothing at the time, but Ama had not wanted to talk too much, especially when she had never actually confided in any of her family.

Jennie heard all about this and showed her sympathy in the way she listened, intermittently just holding Ama's hand. For Ama, she was the first adult who had listened without judgement to Ama pouring out her heart. To be fair, she also found it difficult to speak of her marriage or to identify the real problem. To their children as well as to anyone else. Finally, she was able to let her feelings out without any attempt to spare someone else's feelings. Jennie was truly her friend, and Ama felt a sense of relief being with her.

Both her parents had also died a few years previously, but even if her mother was alive, Ama did not think she would be able to talk to her, as she had never done in the earlier years of marriage. Neither of them would have been any help, Ama thought, as she had done so often before. Complaining about her marriage or about Evans had been out of the question. Ama had made her own bed and it had always been up to her to cope and make the decisions that were required to manage the needs and demands of her marriage and family life. She had chosen the life she wanted, and they had adjusted to it, accepting Evans as a devoted husband.

Ama recalled her father saying that his daughters could always come back home and wondered what he would have said to her now. Her older sister, who was the first to separate from her husband, had found their home a haven for one or two years before going abroad. But then, that marriage was one that they all recognised should not have happened from the start. Of course, there had been no children and no years building up strong bonds and history.

Maybe Ama had waited too long. But when would have been a good time, when there were children being nurtured? Besides, Ama had still been hopeful, believing in the good times rather than the times when she thought she saw Evans and his inability to do better, as he repeatedly promised after any significant conflict.

Peace at any price. Ama had tried to avoid this becoming her reality, even as she suspected that this was Evans' approach. Of course, he would not say that. No, he just lived it as much as he could until the truth became more difficult for him to contain. He did not understand his wife, and it became more and more difficult for him to hide his discontent with what he thought he saw.

As the children grew, it became obvious that he was more focussed on what he wanted, and the marriage became largely just a commitment they must live through. Eventually, it also became more convenient as he depended on the social life that they had managed to create. What would the neighbours say? What would the rest of the family say? What would his siblings say? How would he live on his own? What kind of life could he afford to live?

Ama had also lost sight of who he was and wondered, at times, if she had ever known him.

The sun was going down when the friends finally decided to get up. It had also become really chilly as they collected the few items Ama had brought and moved across to the small flat that she had rented just off the campus. No roommate for her. She had worked hard enough to afford this minor convenience. She dropped everything as Jennie looked around, and they both left again to go out to dinner at a nearby pub.

By this time, the darkness had descended, and the pub was brightly lit. She loved these local pubs. It was such a lively, colourful place, with people chatting at the tables scattered around the room. Behind the counters, people lined up for drinks and to place orders for food – usually burgers and other fast-food items.

This was the place for both women to put the difficulties of the past aside and look forward to a future they would be able to carve out for themselves. The decision was made to look ahead as they drank and shared the platter of tasty bits, laughing at the memories of childhood, travels, and happy times past, and looking forward to possibilities for the days, months, and years ahead.

Chapter Seven

Lying in bed, Ama found it difficult to fall asleep, reflecting on her day and other experiences. Her mind drifted over the events of the last six weeks since she had started her university programme and her new life. It had been eventful in terms of her preoccupation with work and related activities. She thought she was doing better with less time to mull over the last year as she settled into a routine of organising her small flat within a student facility not far off the university campus. She was comfortable knowing that most of the people in the building were students or young professionals. She had made the choice to have a small, compact, almost studio-like apartment instead of sharing with a stranger.

In any case, at her age, she thought it was best to live alone. Age, however, was not an issue that was brought up in this community, where age discrimination was outlawed. Ama felt at home and more than able to keep up in a setting where she more than merited her place. She was making friends – or at least enjoying talking to different people on topical issues, mostly brought together based on mutual interests identified from club membership but also as would be expected to spring up from people from different parts of the country and the world.

Ama had decided to join a social interest club

focussed on writing articles for the university publication. They had organised some evening meet-ups at the local pub, which she had attended a few times. So, she was a familiar face to many people whom she would otherwise have ignored – or been ignored by – on her trek around the campus.

Ama was mostly kept busy with the demands of coursework, with little time to socialise and just enough time to review the path she had taken to this point in her life. She had also crossed paths with some interesting people, judging from the comments that were shared in tutorials. There was a good mix of individuals in her own class – just twenty of them – most nationals, with just Ama and one other person who was an international student.

Most of them were relatively young – under thirty-five years, anyway – with just a few more mature students like Ama. Among them were two ladies and a handsomely more mature gentlemen (or less youthful) who gave the impression of broad experiences from extensive travel. He did not speak often, but when he did, one could not help but listen to his carelessly distinctive tones. He often came in a bit after when everyone was already seated, seeming to be rushing from some other more important event. The lecturer accepted him without question and treated him, in any interaction, almost like a colleague. If Ama had time and interest, she would have investigated further, but she had other things that demanded her attention.

Ama kept in regular contact with Jennie by telephone, but also keeping up their monthly meetings to do something special. With still so much distance to cover between them, either one of them would choose to make the long trek to meet somewhere Ama had never visited. Those meetings were always a lot of fun for them both, despite some moments of melancholia during which Jennie was always full of empathy, filled with reminiscing and laughter about shared memories, and seeking out new experiences.

On one occasion, they had considered some of the activities that were available near Jennie's house. before it got colder. They ended up going to a spa early one morning, followed by a day out shopping in town and then an early dinner before they parted. They each typically travelled after work in the evening to complete a full day together.

Ama realised that Jennie was getting restless with her life which she felt was going nowhere. She seemed to have gotten over the grief of losing both parents in such a short space of time and had started talking about travel to a new foreign destination, trying to get Ama interested enough to join her during her summer break. Ama was not quite sure yet about her next step, finishing this course was what she kept in mind at this stage. She felt she just needed time to feel more like herself – or perhaps to become more at ease with the new person who may have started to evolve.

Ama's children did not contact her often, and she was usually so busy herself, that she had a distraction that helped her resist calling them too often. Things were still a bit sore with her daughter, who saw her father regularly and thought he may be sad about the new path his life had taken. When they last spoke, she was sounding better maybe getting to accept that unexpected events do happen in life and also in the best of families.

But still, there was sometimes little to say once they had gotten over the conversation of the day. Issues like marriage were definitely off the table. Maybe understandably, her mother could no longer give her advice so nothing was shared anywhere close to that area as might have happened naturally in the past. Ama felt like a bit of an outcast in this regard. She even thought of calling Evans at times, but they had agreed that giving each other more time was needed.

Ama reached over for the book on her nightstand. She had not found time to read an action/adventure romance from one of her favourite novelists – a book she had started on her flight but never got time to finish. It was usually a holiday activity in any case and even alone, she reminded herself that her life has not so far been a vacation.

She really had little space for entertainment and changing course from opening the book, Ama decided to engage in some mindfulness exercise instead. She had an early class the next day, and it was already midnight. She had spent more time that she planned on an assignment.

Time to sleep, she thought. Lying on her back and snuggling under her duvet, she focussed on her breath.

Chapter Eight

The phone call came at two a.m. and jolted Ama out of the deep sleep she had finally fallen into – sleep she needed perhaps more than ever in those days of study and still too much reflection, too much room for the regrets she never wanted to entertain. She never waited to question who was at the other end of the line as she tumbled out of bed towards the phone on her dressing table. The room was dark except for the slither of light under the door that helped to orient her to reach out and grab her mobile phone.

She could not see who it was before she called out quickly, *"Hello?"*

The caller was unexpected not calling her by name, she lunged into the explanation for the early morning call, *"Your son's missing!"*

Ama had not heard from her daughter-in-law for at least three years. She had not even attended the last family gathering before she had gotten on the plane, leaving behind the place they had all called home.

"Amelia, hello. What do you mean?" Ama felt her heart pounding in her chest, trying to steady herself for what was to come. Andrew was missing. What could that mean?

Had he finally caved in under the strain of always

being the best at whatever he did? And why was Amelia calling her? Ama had thought they could have been close in those early days, but that had somehow not materialised. They could not manage to get past the strain of Andrew's choice of a young woman who, was in too many ways, not the person everyone had expected him to marry. She was not the professional, even he had expected to be his match.

Amelia had appeared in his life just before he had gone off to law school, pretty and petite, she had worked at the law firm in which he was doing an internship during the holiday after completing his degree. She had found her dream man, it seemed from the start, and he was besotted by her looks and the fact that she looked up to him as the man of her dreams.

Amelia was the girl from story books – long, dark, and curly locks with petite and very attractive physical features. She had woven her way into the family, always friendly and enthusiastic in her efforts to befriend everyone, starting from Evans and Ama. They had initially thought that she was a law student but found out later that she was the receptionist, coming straight from her high school and remaining at the firm ever since. After three years there, it became clear that her only ambition was to find a lawyer as a husband and to become a well-maintained housewife and maybe a mother of one.

This was not what they had expected as a choice Andrew would make, but Ama was happy if it meant that he would be content and more able to relax, letting go of that competitive spirit that seemed to drive him.

Ama had also looked forward to having a daughter-in-law who would provide the grounding her eldest child needed. She had looked forward to them becoming friends up until wedding plans were being made. Amelia's parents were simple, hardworking people, parents of four children, two of whom were still at school.

Andrew was pushed around from the start of the wedding preparations, spending money on the event to satisfy his wife-to-be. Andrew also seemed very protective of Amelia, keeping her apart as much as possible – or so it seemed. Maybe they had both agreed to be the couple who everyone would admire from a safe distance. Ama really did not know, except to realise that she was not the popular visitor she expected to be. With one grandson from the marriage, she had had little occasion to enjoy the family intimacies she imagined.

"Andrew has not been home for the last two nights!" Amelia announced in an angry and perhaps anxious tone.

"Where could he be? And have you called the police?"

"I spoke to him yesterday morning... he apologised for being out so late and said that he was coming home. That was more than twenty-four hours ago?" Amelia's voice was rising and anger seemed to be dominant in her tone.

"I am so fed up with this," she groaned, no doubt in an attempt to let me know how serious the situation had become. Ama, though, was still not sure what was expected of her. What was she able to do and why was Amelia calling her?

Ama remained silent as she considered what to say.

Neither Andrew nor Amelia had even confided in her – or in anyone in the family, as far as she knew. What could she say now? Was Andrew away with another woman? That was the only thing that came to her mind, but of course, this was not something she could say to Amelia. Maybe he had just left his wife and his two-year old son? That did not seem like something Andrew would do. But then, Ama had lost track of her son's ambitions. Much like his father, he seemed to have stopped talking when his life took off.

"Has he done this before, then?" Ama asked tentatively.

"I don't know what is going on with him," Amelia said, apparently ignoring the question. *"He had an office dinner two nights ago and said a few of them were going off for some drinks... I am really fed up. He left me stranded to cope with the shopping for our dinner party this evening. He was supposed to get some steaks for the barbecue. How could he not turn up for this?"*

Ama listened.

"Maybe he will be home soon, then," she said.

There was only silence at the other end until Amelia announced, *"He is not answering when I call his mobile. Maybe he will respond if you call him."*

"What is going on, Amelia? Where is Andrew?" Ama decided that being blunt was the only course of action at this stage. What was there to lose?

"I don't know. Maybe he will tell you... he needs to come home. Please call and tell him to come home," Amelia said before hanging up the phone.

Ama stared at the phone in her hand, wondering what to do next. Should she call Andrew? How would he feel hearing from her at a time like this? Maybe Jon would know what is going on with Andrew. She needed to know something before stepping in. Did Amelia think Andrew was still the child who listened to his mother? What was she really thinking?

She would not be surprised if Jon was not at home, even on a Thursday night. It was after ten p.m. She would try him. At least she would not be waking him up, and the conversation will be an easy one to have. Ama and her last child were quite close and spoke about once each week. As the only unmarried one, he still had room for his mother and without a confidante to listen and give unsolicited advice, welcome or not. At least a confidante who did not expect anything in return.

"Hi, Mom! What's up… it's late by you, isn't it?" Jon was cheerful, as expected at this time of day. Maybe out for drinks with friends?

"Hi, Jon. Yeah, I got an unexpected call that woke me up… where are you?"

"I'm at home, actually… I have a few colleagues over. Who called?" Jon was a bit distracted, as was to be expected.

"From your sister-in-law… wanted me to check on Andrew."

"Hmm, that is strange. Why you?"

"Have you heard from your brother lately? Do you know what he is up to?"

"Not really… he called me a couple weeks ago. Quite

unexpected. He was talking about going out for a drink and finding time for himself. I said he was so tired. Rambling on for a while, I listened but was not really convinced that he needed my help. I mean what can I do for him? He eventually said goodbye after a few minutes of venting."

"What did he vent about? Did he say anything about what is happening at home?"

"Nothing much, really... he did babble on a bit about me enjoying my single life and things like that. Nothing out of the ordinary."

"I am not sure what I am supposed to do... you know Andrew, always the one to be in charge. In the last conversation, he was talking about plans for their dream house."

"Mum, I must go... let me know if there is anything I can do," Jon said quickly before hanging up.

Is this parenting? Always being the one left looking at the phone? Ama thought about her son and knew how she would feel if something bad had happened to him. She dialled his number and listened to the phone ringing until it stopped. Should she try again? Instead, she sent her son a message asking him to get in touch with her urgently. Maybe he would not think Amelia had called her.

Ama had a drink of water, deciding that she should try getting some sleep, but decided that she should call Amelia. Amelia responded in the second ring.

"Amelia, have you heard from Andrew?" she asked calmly.

"No," Amelia answered, not offering any more

information.

Ama felt totally out of her depth. With the geographical distance between them, she knew she was significantly less equipped to deal with this crisis. She told her daughter-in-law to let her know when Andrew was back home before hanging up first this time.

Ama struggled to go back to sleep, but the thoughts of her son, mixed with everything else that had gone on over the last year, did not allow her to escape to the rest that she wanted.

As the light of dawn broke through the trees just beyond her building, creeping through the drawn blinds, she decided to get up. She would shower and dress before she tried to call Andrew again. Maybe he would answer, and she would have time to talk with him before preparing to leave for her first class that day. Thank God it was Friday. At least she would have a bit more time to focus on this problem with Andrew and Amelia.

Ama allowed the phone to ring two, three, four times before she felt she should give up.

"Hello, Mum," the voice that should have been Andrew's was croaky and timid, not the voice she usually heard from her eldest child.

Ama took a deep breath before she answered, *"Andrew, how are you?"*

"I am okay," he responded.

"You are okay? Are you at home?" Ama dared to ask, hoping for the right response. She thought she heard her son's breath as he did not respond for almost twenty seconds.

"I am okay, but I am not at home," he finally said.

Ama checked her time. It was six-thirty a.m., which meant that Andrew's time was two-thirty a.m.

"So, where are you? Are you and Amelia having a night out?" She did not think she should let him know that Amelia had called just yet. She did not know how much he was willing to tell her at that point.

Again, Andrew seemed to think before he chose what to say next.

"No, Amelia is not with me. I have not been home for the last two days," he finally said.

Ama chose her next words carefully. She could not risk having him drop off from the call without talking to her.

"How is that? You want to tell me where you are then, or why you are not at home?"

Again, there was silence on the line, longer than previously. Ama heard another deep breath from her son before he seemed to make up his mind to speak.

"I left them, Mum. I left Amelia. I couldn't take it any more... it just became too much..."

"Does Amelia know you left her? Did you tell her this?" I asked carefully.

"No," he answered. *"I left two evenings ago for a drink with colleagues and have not returned since... I just made up my mind..."*

"So, what is your plan? What do you plan to do next? You need to go home and speak with her at some point, and it is better to do this sooner. Remember, it is not just the two of you to consider. You also have responsibility for

Adrian. You have clothes? Where are you staying?"

Ama heard another deep breath. This time it had a tone of relief. Ama thought he must be relieved to be able to tell her – or someone who cared about him – what was going on. That made her feel better. Her son was alive and talking to her. They would be able to sort this out. Of course, they would, she thought.

When Ama finally got off the phone to Andrew, he was sounding a lot better. He said that he was going to try to sleep a couple hours if he could before leaving to go home to talk with Amelia. He had been at a shabby motel, mostly drinking after the first long night out. He was happy to leave that place.

Ama had promised Andrew that she would be there for him. He had to decide, after talking to Amelia, what he was going to be doing, but she was there if he needed to talk a bit more or other support. Maybe he needed some time out, like a trip to somewhere offering a change of pace for a while. He had holidays due from his firm.

Some time out might be just what he needed to feel refreshed before he made any final decision that would also affect the life of his young son. He promised to call her in a couple of days. He said he was feeling better and thanked her for helping. She reminded him that she loved him and that he was not alone. She would accept whatever he decided, as parents had to do with grown children. This was his life and his decision.

She did not know what was best for him and could only hope and pray that he found it.

Before preparing her breakfast and leaving the house,

Ama felt she needed a few minutes to reflect and get herself into a calm space. She was ready to face the day about thirty minutes later, locking the door of her tiny apartment and taking a brisk walk across the tree-lined avenue and onto the university campus about one kilometre away.

Everything will be okay, she told herself. Life leads us in unexpected places, but we will be okay.

Her mind shifted to her first class and the presentation she had prepared. She was looking forward to it. This was a small part of a group presentation and was her area of expertise – a report on an intervention she had used with a small group of children with anxiety issues.

Chapter Nine

Saturday morning was not much different for Ama. She woke before her alarm could sound, a bit earlier than she normally would, especially after the week she had and a late night. Thoughts of Andrew and Amelia flickered in her mind, along with those of different encounters she had had during the week on her mind. She had not yet spoken to Amelia, not calling again, and Amelia had not called her. For a brief moment, she wondered if she should call as she got ready for her day, checking the weather forecast before deciding what she was going to wear. Amelia had promised to call, but maybe Andrew had said that they had spoken.

She had time to take a leisurely shower enjoying the warm water before going to prepare her breakfast and meal for lunch. She tried not to depend on the cafeteria food, as she left eating out for times when she was tired of the routine and felt a break was well-deserved and really necessary. She had two tutorial sessions that morning but was free the rest of the day – free to do individual study and anything else she had planned. She would make time to call Andrew or Amelia when she returned at lunchtime, when they would be sure to be awake, hopefully with Andrew back home as he had promised.

Ama got no answer from either of their phones. It

seemed obvious that Amelia and Andrew were together again. That after all, was what they did together… wasn't it? She shook her head, trying to shake off the feeling of disappointment this evoked. Let her not go off in this direction. Maybe she could find out if Jon had heard anything, or should she just let it go? She took two deep breaths as she decided to let go – they were both adults, after all. Either one will call when they are ready. Let her just leave it to them. She dismissed any lingering doubt, and telling herself that her son was safe, she organised her study session that would stretch into the late evening. Everyone will be fine, she thought one last time before her focus shifted to the research theories she was using in her latest assignment.

The hours flew by as Ama worked, getting up only when her alarm went off. She had set it for a walk at three-thirty p.m. The time allowed her to have the few remaining minutes of daylight, a time she especially enjoyed. On return, she would prepare a light dinner, thinking of the available options for the evening. Should she study some more, read, watch a movie, call Jennie perhaps? Or maybe she should try something different. She had promised herself that she would go out sometime in the evening. Why not try the new pub that so many people on campus liked to hang out at?

She should not have a wait for company, should she? Her team mates for the last group assignment had issued a tentative invitation, but she knew that they were unsure, given the obvious age difference between her and most of her classmates. She smiled over this, understanding some of their confusion – to be not so long from home, under parents, and meeting an adult who might seem a bit cool, like a regular student. Maybe she would do something different that evening. Ama smiled again. That will be a first. She tended to make great plans or at least to have thoughts of doing great things. Many of them actually remained in her mind or sometimes in the little book where she sometimes wrote down things she would like to do.

Ama returned from her walk along the riverbank, which was not more than a fifteen-minute walk from where she lived, in the opposite direction from the high street and university. After a few minutes in the shower, she felt a wave of excitement, thinking she would go to the pub that evening. Why not? She was in the mood for some fun, a bit of joviality that did not depend on anyone else – well, at least not on someone going with her.

Ama opened her closet, looking for the right outfit that would say, *I know I am not young but I am a semi-attractive woman in my middle years, just out for some fun.* She smiled... this was not bad at all. She chose a woollen sweater that she had bought with Jennie. It fitted her slim frame over a pair of fitted jeans worn over tights and high-heeled ankle boots. This seemed fine for a chilly evening, she thought, as she added a pair of looped earrings and let down her braided hair. Ama wore very little make-up when she had to do it herself, which was usually outside her children's weddings when special treatment had been provided. She chose her going-out coat of leather with a wool lining around the neck and slung a long-strapped little bag across chest just before leaving her flat.

Whatever happened, she was looking forward to enjoying her first solo evening out.

It was not a long walk to the pub, and the evening was pleasant. In under twelve minutes, she had arrived. The street was busy on a Saturday night with lots of places well-lit, and the pub was easy to find. *The Blazing Sun,* the sign read. She wondered if the owner had travelled much to far-off tropical places. She did not associate her new home with much in terms of sunshine, but maybe this pub was a place of dreams. She laughed at her frivolity as she pushed open the door of *The Blazing Sun*, feeling the ambience of the place with soft music in the background. There were areas of bright light, particularly around the bar, with some more subdued lighting in the corners of the seating area.

Ama heard laughter and a lot of chatter coming from different directions. It was not overcrowded in any way, but there was a fairly large number of patrons, with most tables already taken. She instinctively looked to see if there were other people on their own but did not have time to catch a glimpse of any before she spied the group of her groupmates. They were actually there, she thought, but thought twice about possibly intruding. *Should she join them?* She wondered, but this was taken out of her hands as she did not have time to look away. One of them, Patricia, had seen her and quickly alerted the others who raised their hands or looked towards her with welcoming smiles. She heard her name as she drew near to the table, as they all shuffled around to make room for her.

Ama was not normally shy with people and threw aside threads of any social anxiety as her eyes moved around the small group. Four of them were from her team, but there were two others – one, a woman maybe a bit older than the others, and interestingly, the mysterious classmate, the somewhat ruggedly handsome man who had invariably made an entrance to lectures. What was his name? She was sure she had heard it at least once. "And this is Mathew – Matt to his friends." She heard Anthony (Tony), who was doing the introductions, say. "Matt, this is Ama." Ama smiled as she responded, reaching out her hand to take his that was already outstretched.

"And this is Paula… she is also in our class." Ama shifted her gaze to the woman sitting next to Matt.

"Hi, Paula… I am Ama," she said.

The two women exchanged smiles and greetings as Ama found the empty chair around the table.

"What are you drinking?" Peter, who seemed to have taken on the role of host, asked Ama as she settled in. They had a small assortment of drinks on the table, and Ama chose a cider. She did not know what the arrangement was for drinks but felt that she would catch on at some point. The conversation quickly resumed with James, a burly and fresh-faced youth in his late twenties, filling Ama in on the topic before everyone turned to ask her opinion. It was a somewhat typical psychology-related evening discussion – what drew people together: similarities or differences. Ama was not ready to commit to an answer as she guided the question to the general position.

There was a lot of humour in that group, and Ama felt

herself relaxing as she listened and joined in with brief comments or queries to the more talkative members. Besides Peter and Tony, there were Michelle and Ava from the team. Michelle presented like the more stereotypical Psychology nerd, a full head of mousy-coloured strands falling around her face with large-sized spectacles, but with an energetic manner and sharp wit. Michelle always had ideas for the group. Ava was more subdued and may have been a primary-level teacher before choosing to pursue Psychology. She came across as very straightforward in her opinions. She seemed more relaxed tonight than Ama had ever seen her over the few weeks of working together. Ama thought she may have been a lot like Ava when she was young, though perhaps less serious. Ava took learning very seriously.

Peter and Tony may not be what others expected in Masters-level Psychology students and seemed somewhat laid-back, though in different ways. Peter was the sports-minded male with an authoritative streak, wanting to get things done without taking it too seriously. He was the one to lighten the atmosphere when everyone else seemed too tense. Tony was also atypical. He may never have expected himself to reach this far in any education and was the first of his family to do so. Tony was less confident in his opinions but also there to do his part to succeed. He was a sweetheart, very funny, usually with a joke, and very kind.

During the evening, Ama caught Matt's eyes a few times. He seemed interested in her, with noticeable glimpses that she was aware of even while not looking towards him. They sat with Michelle and Tony between them, so were almost across from each other. There was no opportunity for any direct conversation, but their opinions at times clashed on various topics of conversation, usually ending with a laugh or comment about follow-up at a later time. Ama did not learn much about Matt during this encounter – not unexpected in that setting – but at least heard his voice, somewhat deep tones with an underlying resonance of feelings akin to solemnity or harsh lessons learned covered in humour. She could not decide, of course, but the sense of mystery deepened. Ama thought that Matt's eyes were kind, with a slight twinkle, maybe, and almost giggled at herself. In any case, he did not seem jaded or cynical, which was good. Good for what, she asked herself, shaking away the reverie as she paid attention to the latest topic.

Ama had hoped for some dancing, but of course, that may not be the way of pubs. She did not really think it was and decided that maybe she will go to somewhere with dancing next. She always enjoyed dancing and had not done any of this for some time, not even when alone, as she had done before. The evening passed with a lot of drinking, though alongside an informal dinner menu that was a combination of fast food and more typical restaurant fare, and a lot of conversation with hardly a moment of silence.

Persons sitting next to each other engaged in intermittent dialogue during space in general conversation during the meal, but otherwise, there was no time for anything bordering intimate or personal exchanges. Ama did not think anyone was a couple, although she had thought that Tony and Michelle seemed to like each other, though not dating. In any case, these were early days still in the first semester of the two-year programme. She thought though, that they would have to make haste if the attraction was mutual, as they were each expected to go off to practicums in different places after the second semester and most of Year 2. She had not yet decided where she was going.

It was almost midnight when the evening ended with mutual consensus about the need for sleep. A few of them had definitely drunk a bit too much, causing some tipsiness. Not a drinker, Ama was as clear-headed as when she came in but with definite sparks of joy and satisfaction from the evening. She was tired, though, and was looking forward to lying on her bed with some awake time to think over the evening of such friendly banter and shared enjoyment. She wondered if this was usually how it was. Also, if it was just her experience. Everyone did seem to have a good time, though, as they shared goodbyes breaking up at the door.

Ama walked at a slow pace with Peter, Matt, and Michelle for about ten minutes before she needed to turn the corner for another block before her flat. There was some question about her walking the short distance alone, and Matt chose to walk with her as it was just a small detour to his flat. Of course, they were almost neighbours… few people lived far away from the campus.

There was silence for a few seconds as Matt and Ama walked, a trifle uncomfortable maybe for Ama, first real silence for the evening, and with her mysterious classmate. She laughed to herself, then looking up to see him looking her way. They both smiled before starting to say something almost simultaneously.

"You first," Matt said, laughter in his tone.

"It was a nice evening," Ama said, saying the most obvious to break the silence.

"This is my first time going out and I really enjoyed it."

Matt seemed a bit intrigued by that, looking at her intently.

"Is it? It was also my first time going out with anyone. But yes, it was a nice evening. They are a nice bunch."

"We have been team mates over the semester, working quite well together. They have invited me before, but… you know… not sure I will fit in…" She glanced at him with a smile. "You know, thinking they were just being polite… not sure about the socialising…"

"Yes, I know. I don't socialise very much myself. Always too busy… but also aware that I am one of the mature students… not always sure how it fits for socialising," Matt spoke quietly, sounding slightly introspective.

"Well, here I am. I live here." Matt was a few centimetres taller than Ama and she looked up with a smile as they stood more closely together. "Thanks for walking with me, especially my first time being out so late," Ama spoke with a somewhat deprecating giggle.

"You're welcome, Ama. I enjoyed meeting you. I hope we will both be willing to do it again."

Matt and Ama smiled at each other, exchanging goodbyes before she briskly walked the few yards, entering the main entrance to her flat with a slight wave as she closed the door. Yes, Matt was still standing there waiting for her to enter safely. He was a gentleman, Ama thought with a big smile.

Chapter Ten

Ama did not know if it was by design and, if so, whose design, but in the weeks after this first real meeting, she and Matt always managed to be sitting not far from the other, exchanging greetings or smiles from a distance or brief exchanges in the corridor as they went about their different activities. There was no time for more, as both seemed busy with their lives. Ama wondered about his activities and his life – did he have a family nearby?

Ama went about her usual activities, also thinking about her children at certain times. Neither Amelia nor Andrew called to follow up on recent happenings, with conversations falling into their usual pattern of disengagement. She eventually called Andrew, asking how he was. He dismissed any real sharing on his decision but did say that he and Amelia were doing well and were managing with family issues. He had sounded well enough, and Ama did not push for anything more. She had to accept that this was sometimes how it was with grown children. Parents did not have to be included in the intimate details of their lives. She kept up her usual intermittent texts, also asking about her grandson, and left them to their lives as she manoeuvred a way through her own.

Ama heard regularly from Jon, but conversation with

Susan was not much different from those with Andrew. She kept up enquiries about the children and had some chats with them directly. With Jon, she got regular updates about activities he chose to share, especially when he needed some advice. Otherwise, he just checked in because Ama had insisted, as he was the only one without a family, and she sometimes worried if she did not hear from him.

Ama did not get in touch with her ex-husband, and there was barely any mention of him from the children except for an unintentional bit of information when he visited or they visited him. This was not happening often, as Evans had never had much to share. He would engage and visit with the grandchildren when he was ready. Everybody seemed well, and Ama was happy that there was no more family drama. Hopefully, this would not be broken for some time, giving them a chance to heal from the significant change over the last two years. Jennie had been quiet for some time, and their regular meetings had fallen off a bit, partly because Ama was also preoccupied with studies and the extra work she placed on herself to be able to keep up.

It was the last class of the autumn semester when Ama and Matt actually got together. Ama had been thinking about what she would be doing over the two-week break, particularly for Christmas, but had not made any plans. She had met with Jennie on one occasion over the last month, but Jennie had not been in her usual jovial mood for weeks, seeming lost without the support she had sometimes relied on from her parents in the background.

She had not spoken again about travelling, which she had done a lot of, even with her parents alive. Jennie was unsure about what she would be doing for her first Christmas without them, but Ama felt that she would just show up and help cheer up her friend, who had been there for her when she had felt most alone. She would call Jennie and arrange a shopping trip for Christmas and would be happy to stay over by Jennie for at least the two days from Christmas Eve. Most of her classmates, including the members of the small team she had worked with over the semester, had flights heading home or to other places with family and friends. They had had informal goodbyes over the last couple of days.

Ama had not seen Matt since the week before and wondered what was going on with him. He had been there for the three exams but had not attended the closing group sessions. She was walking slowly, shuffling through her hold-all with her head bent.

Somehow, she always had difficulty finding her phone… better she called Jennie to talk while she walked to her flat. She was so engrossed in trying to get a hold of her elusive phone that she almost bumped into someone coming in her direction. Looking up quickly, she realised it was Matt. He was smiling at her, not surprised at all.

"Hi, Ama," he said; *his expression a combination of joviality and earnestness,* she thought.

"Hi, Matt," Ama responded, a bit breathless. She thought her voice sounded that way – maybe it was from the effort of trying to locate her phone, or maybe it may have something to do with Matt's unexpected appearance.

Matt and Ama both stood in a moment of slightly awkward silence as they just looked at each other, before a little burst of laughter as they started to speak at the same time.

"You go first," Ama said, looking up at him expectantly.

"No," said Matt more decisively now. "You go," with a smile.

"I was actually just going to say that my missing phone was taking up my attention," Ama said.

"Go ahead," Matt responded. "Have you found it?"

"This can take me some time, a common occurrence," said Ama. "I'm sure it is in there. I'll find it later. There's no rush. I was just going to call a friend, but you are here now." Ama looked at him, realising that she was happy to have almost bumped into him. But on paying attention, thought he seemed to be on a mission.

"I actually came this way with the hope of bumping into you," Matt announced somewhat bashfully for him. He looked at her, trying to read her expression before going on. "I know we have not had much time to really get to know each other, but I know you are almost alone here and wondered if you had plans for Christmas. Or maybe we can do something… together, I mean."

Ama was not expecting this at all. Had she made such an impression on him that he wanted to spend time with her? She also knew very little about him. Nothing much, really. He just seemed to have more going on than just university classes, unlike her. She had wondered if he had a family – a wife or children somewhere.

Ama looked at him, waiting for some signal about how to respond. Finding none, she decided to be honest.

"I actually have no plans at all. Was thinking though of making some with my only friend here…" she spoke tentatively.

"So you will be busy then?" Matt looked a trifle disappointed, Ama thought.

"No, not really; my girlfriend recently lost her parents, who she had been caring for, and has been a bit down. I was looking for my phone to call her just now… I have not been the best friend, being more preoccupied with university and my own activities over the last few weeks." Ama stopped talking and took a deep breath.

"I would like to make some plans with you," Ama said and was repaid with a wide smile from Matt.

"You're sure? That's good, although I don't want to take you away fully from your girlfriend."

"I will call her when I get home. I was hoping she and I could do some Christmas shopping and maybe stay over for Christmas Day. What did you have in mind for us to do?" she asked.

"Are you free for dinner tomorrow, maybe? We can meet and get to know each other a bit then. Decide then?"

"I would love that," answered Ama.

"So, what about meeting at the same place at six?" Matt stood waiting for Ama's agreement before they started walking together.

"I can do that." Ama smiled, and Matt smiled.

As they walked, Ama and Matt talked about the end of the

semester, with Matt also telling her that he had a family commitment that occupied him over the last week. He did not explain what the commitment involved, but Ama looked forward to hearing more from him when they met. There was a lot she wanted to find out about Matt, and she thought that dinner with him was a good start.

Matt, on his part, paid attention to the way Ama spoke and thought how much he was attracted to her voice and her smile. He really wanted to get to know her, including what had led her to pursue this university programme all alone. Did she have a husband somewhere? Children? He was looking forward to getting to know her better.

Matt and Ama slowed to a stop when they reached outside the gates just after the street to Ama's apartment. He remembered where she lived from the last occasion when he had walked her home. He hoped to repeat this in the future but decided to leave her to get home and make plans with her friend. He will wait until tomorrow.

"Well, see you tomorrow, Matt," Ama said looking at him.

"I look forward to seeing you, Ama," said Matt. "Have a good evening."

Ama and Matt said goodbye to each other and walked off in different directions. Ama did not want Matt to see her looking back but ended up doing so at the same moment that he did. Another wave and a smile were shared as they walked on, both thinking of their meeting the next day.

Ama held in her excitement until she reached her tiny apartment just off the block of university residences. Once indoors, she gave the skip and swirl that she had held in. A laugh followed as she told herself that she felt like a teenager again. What exactly was she hoping for, really? She did not know, but she felt good with the anticipation of a date with a handsome man, her mysterious classmate. It reminded her that she had to call Jennie, especially now she had some news to share. She searched her bag looking for her phone, giving her time to rethink sharing her excitement with her friend, who had not been so happy lately.

Finding her phone, which somehow always seemed hard to locate among the things she carried around in her bag, Ama stretched out on her bed and called Jennie. It was early evening, but Ama believed that her friend was likely to be at home, as the school term had ended a week earlier.

The phone gave about three rings before she heard Jennie's voice at the other end, saying hello to her friend and sounding more than a bit happier than she had in a while.

"Hi, Ama," she said. *"You have finally come up for air! Did you have your last class today?"*

"Hi, Jennie," Ama answered. *"Yes, and it's a relief to have a bit of freedom for a couple of weeks. Of course, the first thing I started thinking about was Christmas and what are your plans. Can we do something? Go shopping, organise something for Christmas Day…"*

"Well, shopping sounds great… it will give me time to share my news as well…" Jennie answered.

"Not too sure about Christmas Day, though, but let's meet… when do you think? On Saturday… you want to

come up to me? We can do our shopping at your favourite mall."

"That sounds good. You sound good. I am looking forward to your news!" Ama said.

"Can you give me a hint?"

Jennie laughed, and Ama was happy to hear it.

"You can wait. Things are better, and I look forward to sharing with my friend. See you on Saturday... let's meet early, about nine a.m. Unless you want to come on Friday evening and stay overnight."

"No, actually I have something on Friday. I will take the early train on Saturday morning."

The friends agreed and they hung up. Ama was intrigued by Jennie's news. It seemed they both had something good to share based on Jennie's upbeat manner.

Chapter Eleven

Ama turned in her bed, opening her eyes slowly to see a hint of sunlight peeking through the thick curtains at her bedroom window. She liked the idea of having a view of the skyline, not being totally blocked off from the natural environment. Her flat was fully self-contained in a block of apartments within a larger area of buildings – a lot of them buildings that were available as housing for university students and staff. Others were business blocks, including stores and other utility services that made her location a very convenient place to live.

Ama's view of the sky allowed her to have a first look at what the weather was like. The heating had already come on, and with light outside, she realised that she had slept past her normal wake-up time. She had remembered to turn off her alarm at the end of classes the previous day. She reached out for her phone, checking the weather forecast for the day as she remembered the date with Matt.

The anticipation of spending time with Matt brought back the pleasant, gleeful response, but it was now accompanied by some nerves, and self-doubt about what path she was taking. She had not really thought about dating, especially so soon after the…

Divorce… she still found it hard even to say the word. The end of her marriage had been so unexpected, even after the challenges and possibility of this outcome that had been referred to a number of times in her and Evans' arguments. It was not something she had planned on, definitely had not kept it in mind. Those feelings dampened what she felt was otherwise a good time in her life. Would she ever be able to shake the second- guessing of her choice, inexplicably creeping up at times into her awareness, encroaching on what should be happy moments?

Ama focussed her attention back to the weather – outside looked promising, and she would not like the day to be rainy for her meeting with Matt. She smiled broadly just thinking about it and began to think about preparations for this major event! So great that the weather forecast was good for the entire day, generally to be a bright day and evening despite the temperatures close to single numbers – lowest eleven degrees C. That was a good sign, wasn't it? Ama was getting used to these temperatures since she knew now how to dress to keep warm.

What was she going to wear? She stopped herself with a deep breath. What was happening to her? It was just a meeting of two people who wanted to spend some time getting to know each other outside of the classroom, she told herself before she could get carried away. She chastised herself for the adolescent bubble of feelings that threatened to take over the reality of a common adult activity – friends meeting for a drink or dinner.

The evening before, after speaking with Jennie and making plans for their shopping trip, had been spent talking with Jon, who had called just as she sat down with her dinner.

She had taken a lot of time organising her course

material and equipment, planning to take most of the two weeks off work. She deserved it, she knew, but her son had been in a talkative mood which included stories about a new girl – nothing new there. She had been too tired to do much after this conversation, lasting over two hours, and fell asleep almost as soon as she was in bed and under her covers.

Ama told herself that she did not need to go shopping for anything new. It was not necessary, as she had more than suitable clothing in her closet. She just needed to be sensible about the meeting (or date!) with Matt and to choose something. Forget that it was her first date in more than thirty years. She had not been on many of those in her life, had she? She had met and married Evans at such a young age, she had had very few dates, actually, and none as a real adult. This was a significant event, she realised. But still, much better not to over-romanticise it. She wished then that she could have spoken to Jennie about it before this evening. She did not recall really even mentioning him in conversation with her friend – there had been no real need to do that and no occasion particularly within the last few weeks.

Ama accepted that she would have to manoeuvre her way through this on her own. Nobody to tell, she accepted, as she opened her closet. She did not see much to choose from there and remembered a suitcase with a few outfits she had not had occasion to wear. No dress-up had been needed for her limited social activities. Ama took out the clothing she found, laying them on her bed, planning to try on and decide what she was going to wear.

Chapter Twelve

Matt had lived most of his early life in a village that seemed huge compared to where Ama had lived most of her own life. From what he described, it was a place of sloping hills and sprawling farmland, along with rocky cliffs overlooking a pristine seaside, uncontaminated by the influx of foreigners usually led by a tourist trade. Matt grew up seeing his parents at work on what would have been one of the smaller farms in the neighbourhood that involved the rearing of domestic animals, including cows and poultry, but also growing fields of vegetable crops. They hired a few persons at times to assist, but it had been a family-run business that they had bought together when the original owners were selling off small portions of their land space. Ellie and Phil had been just in time to secure that bit of land for themselves.
They had not been local people having themselves met only about two years earlier, young people who had been backpacking from their own countries and had found each other. As he skimmed over their story, it sounded like a fairy tale to Ama, listening with real interest as he spoke.

Matt was the eldest of their children, with two younger sisters. He had spent his time scoring the beaches when not occupied with school or on the farm doing the chores set out by his parents, particularly for him as the eldest and only male child. It had not been too much, and Matt had generally enjoyed the work, especially with the animals. He developed an early interest in their care, which had led to his first career choice – veterinary medicine.

School had been just a few miles away, and Matt, and eventually his sisters who were seven and ten years younger, travelled to and from school on the bus, leaving his parents to get on with their work on the farm. He had not been a bad student as he told it and made a lot of friends, one of whom he would eventually marry after they both finished college in a nearby county.

That early marriage had not been a surprise to anyone, as they had been a twosome throughout high school after knowing each other for most of their lives. Their families had been friends and neighbours, and they had a lot of shared memories. Once Matt had settled into the teenaged phase, being one of the more popular boys playing on the football team and managing to be a good student, he decided that he more than just liked being with Sarah. The attraction between them had developed without them being fully aware of it.

They had enjoyed activities with mutual friends, and the years led into going to nearby college and making the decision to marry once they had graduated and secured jobs. Matt's first job was in a small veterinary clinic in a nearby town, where he could still support his aging parents with the animal care while Sarah taught English at the high school.

They had had their second child, who was three years old when tragedy struck. Sarah was diagnosed with ovarian cancer and passed away before her daughter's fourth birthday. As expected, Matt had been devastated, catapulted into grief and not being able to make sense of the turn that his life had taken. He did not feel that anything in his life had prepared him for this catastrophic event. He had walked around in a daze for months, barely managing to get himself to work, that was second nature to him, but not doing such a good job in caring for Marie and Alan, who was six years older than his sister. Matt and Sarah had been married for eleven years when she died.

Ama felt herself drawn into Matt's story, her own experiences feeling like so much less in terms of the grief that she knew he would have carried for a long time after. She felt that she should offer some kind of comfort but realised that not only were they not close enough for the expression of support she wished she could give, but Matt had gone on speaking, simply sharing his story to introduce himself to her. He had had the last eighteen years to have gotten past that grief, gradually adapting to being a single parent while occupied with his veterinary practice that had taken unexpected turns.

Chapter Thirteen

Ama had prepared herself for her date with Matt, finding an outfit: a grey pair of slacks with a white silk blouse that she favoured, contributing to a casual elegance with accessories of merging colours that complimented her outfit. She wore this under her dark grey coat and black calf-length boots. She thought, as she arrived at the pub where Matt was already waiting, how easy it was for men. Matt was casually dressed in pants of a similar colour as hers and a black jumper. He looked tall and handsome… and quite serious, she thought.

Matt smiled when he looked up and saw her approaching. Ama had been relieved to see that smile that lightened the contours of his face, and she wondered what he had been thinking up to that moment. Had he been regretting his decision to seek her out for them to get to know each other? She loved his curly hair that was kept short enough to be neat. He had streaks of grey closer to his sideburn and a closely shaved beard. Ama had not reached the stage where she was comfortable seeing strands of grey appearing in her own hair and was definitely not prepared to show it. She knew her mother had started becoming grey before she was forty, which she had always thought to be a nuisance. She knew things were a bit different now, as many older women seemed to embrace their greying locks, but she felt that this was not for everybody. Some people seemed to look attractive, while others just looked... well... older. She felt she might be in the latter group – or maybe it was just vanity that had passed down from her grandmother, who up to her ninetieth birthday, continued to hide her grey locks. That was really so funny, if you think about it, Ama thought, covering her smile in the seconds being reaching Matt, standing near a stool at the bar.

Matt reached out his arm to greet her, taking her hand in his for a brief moment as he looked directly at her in greeting. He looked so confident, Ama thought, while she was just a tiny bit more nervous than she thought she should be. She did manage to smile – not just derisively at herself this time, as she was genuinely happy to see him.

"Hello, Matt," she said, responding to his use of her name as well in greeting.

"I am happy to see you," Matt said. "I was just wondering whether you had changed your mind..."

Ama thought then, with some relief, that that might explain his very serious experience just before he saw her. It was good to know that he may have also been a bit nervous about their date – not quite the suave and confident man he might appear to be. Some shared vulnerability was always welcome.

"Oh no, I wouldn't do that," she said, feeling more relaxed.

Matt had been waiting where he could have a view of the

entrance, but together they decided on where they wanted to sit. The pub was still relatively empty, as they had arrived a bit earlier ahead of the crowd that was normally expected at this popular meeting place for adults of varying ages. The younger and middle-aged crowd came after work, but there were a few who had chosen this place for an evening out, couples on date night.

Matt and Ama found a seat in one of the more secluded and cosier spaces, away from the steady movement of persons to and from the bar, leaving or entering. They thought that provided the ideal setting for them to talk and get to know each other. Matt had held his jacket over his arm and reached forward to help Ama take off her own. She felt a moment of pleasure that he was such a gentleman and wondered if most men still did this. This was definitely new territory for her, as she had not had anything even close to a date in nearly thirty years, not counting evenings out with Evans. This was really new, and she had not considered what would be different and actually, what was expected, in her focus on Matt himself.

Matt and Ama may have faced a similar reality at the same time as they both sat facing the other. Some moments of silence passed before they both gave a slightly nervous laugh. This seemed to clear the tension that had inevitably built up with this first meeting alone. They spoke almost at the same time before another laugh. This seemed to happen to them a lot, even in such a short acquaintance.

"You first," Matt said.

"I am just thinking that I have not been out on a date in a while," Ama said, deciding to begin with honesty.

"Well, you are not alone," Matt said quickly, with a slight smile.

Talking to each other was not difficult, and the conversation about their lives and interests flowed after this. It started with their mutual interest in Psychology/Psychotherapy, and there was barely any silence except for the mutual pauses over their meal.

The evening passed quickly, and it was after midnight when Matt left Ama at the entrance of her flat. They were both happy with the time they had spent together, and though there was no commitment to see each other during the Christmas, they both recognised a connection that meant they would see each other again. Matt reached out and gave Ama a gentlemanly kiss on her cheek. Ama thought that she had stopped breathing for part of a second. She smiled as they looked closely at each other before she turned to open her door with Matt waiting to see her safely inside. Ama knew, as perhaps Matt also did, that this was a generally safe neighbourhood, with people walking around at different hours without mishap, but she appreciated the gesture. Once inside, she gave him a wave as she moved up the stairs, seeing him turning away with a glance to her side.

Chapter Fourteen

Ama had overslept, forgetting to set her alarm after her date with Matt. When she had arrived in her flat, she had moved around in a bit of a glow, too dreamy-eyed like a teenager rather than a woman who was approaching her fiftieth birthday. She had stopped to realise that maybe she was older than Matt, working on the timelines in his story.

Neither of them had asked directly about age.

Ama had a bit of a scamper getting to the train station, not wanting to be late for her day out with Jennie. The plan was to include Christmas shopping, but they also had a lot of catching up to do. As she sat on the train for the hour-long journey, she had time to think about her friend, hoping that she was feeling better about the change in her life without her parents. Jennie had always been such a cheerful person, always with a lot going on in her life, with an enjoyment for travelling and being a great support to others, including Ama.

Jennie was a born teacher, really loving her job. They had shared that with each other, but unlike Ama, Jennie had had the time to enjoy other adventures, which she had no doubt brought to the classroom. Her good cheer, creativity, and adventurous spirit enhanced her interaction with those around her. Ama was so happy that they were friends knowing that without Jennie, she would hardly have ventured out to leave the home she had known all her life to take on this new chapter. Ama's adventurous spirit had not taken on the wings to fly over the last thirty years. She was now looking forward to opening the pages of this new book on her life, thanks to Jennie.

Getting off at the train station in Jennie's hometown, Ama decided that she would take a taxi – in the weeks of summer, during her early visits, she had followed Jennie's lead and often taken the twenty-minute trek on foot unless it was rainy, but this time, she was anxious to reach Jennie. Besides, it was so far a cloudy morning with temperatures to match at this time in December.

As the taxi drove up to Jennie's house – where she had moved back to live with her parents in the last few months, staying there since their deaths just months apart – Ama was a bit taken aback as her friend came rushing out the door, just in time for them to greet each other when the taxi stopped. She was just like the old Jennie as they hugged. Had it been so long since Ama had seen her friend? Jennie was enthusiastic, to help Ama with her overnight bag as the friends entered the house.

"What took you so long!" Jennie said with a youthful giggle as she ushered her friend into the living room.

Ama took a good look at Jennie, trying to work out what had changed so significantly in her friend's life. It had not been so long since she had seen her. It had only been a few weeks – four, to be exact. Yes, she had seen her friend a few times and they had continued talking; While Ama had been busy with work to visit as the semester entered the last leg. Jennie had seemed to drop off the grid. Well, maybe Ama had as well...

"Well, I did have a late night out... but I do need to ask, how you are doing?" Ama responded. She would share her updates after hearing from Jennie.

"I met someone," Jennie spoke quickly, "and we are moving to New Zealand!"

"What are you saying?" Ama had not expected anything like this.

"I met someone – a most unexpected event... I still cannot believe it myself," Jennie said, laughing but with an intense look, trying to assess her friend's thoughts. Ama held on to her friend's hands, looking at her and seeing a bit of fear mixed with joy and happiness. She really needed to get her friend's support, and Ama knew that this was the time to be the person Jennie needed.

"Tell me about this person... and what I am hearing about New Zealand. Sounds really exciting!"

Ama listened to Jennie telling her about the man she had met, just by chance, literally bumping into each other at the supermarket. Jennie had been doing her weekly shopping and trying to reach to an upper shelf for a box of her favourite chocolates.

Someone seemed to have put it away to hide it, maybe, as there was no more in the normal place. Ama knew of her friend's addiction to chocolate, particularly when she was not feeling at her best. It was her comfort food.

Anyway, Jennie was on tiptoes reaching for the box when she got momentarily distracted by a noise nearby which may have caused her to lose her balance slightly, causing the chocolate to slip and topple over. Jennie, not quite steady, moved quickly to catch it, only to clash with the man now nearby, standing over his trolley. It seemed to be one of those moments from a romance movie, the way Jennie told it, a smile of unbelief plastered across her face.

Ama did not have time to ask any questions as Jennie recalled what happened next between herself and this man – now identified as Peter and the person she would, in one month's time, be following across the world. Jennie wanted to know that she was not being impulsive and about to make the worst mistake of her life. She was far from the age of teenage crushes and following dreams. She had had a couple more serious relationships in her life but nothing that had produced any feelings as the ones she was now aware of. These feelings had catapulted her into making a decision that would bring such a significant change to her life.

Having time to reflect as Jennie spoke, Ama thought that her friend may have been preparing for this day throughout her life. She had always been happy travelling to new places, but they had turned out only as holidays, with no reason to make serious changes to her stable lifestyle, including her teaching career. Relationships at home had lasted months, and one even a couple of years, but eventually, they had ended – with some disappointed for Jennie but no real heartbreak.

The death of her parents may have been the turning point for Jennie, as she had never seen herself being able to move away from them, particularly as their only child. She was the one to take care of them and could not ever be far away.

When Jennie stopped for air, having shared mostly everything with her friend, Ama did not have much to ask except to have additional confirmation of the feelings that Jennie had developed for Peter and more about what Peter was like that most attracted Jennie to make such a quick decision.

Peter was a middle-aged father of two grown children who were married and lived in the same city. His wife had died about ten years previously, and this had been his first trip abroad to reconnect with a brother he had not seen in a number of years. Jennie was hoping to arrange an evening out for Ama to meet him, and of course, Ama was excited to do this.

Ama was able to stay over the few days until Christmas, getting a chance to know Peter and, also, she thought, for Jennie to be more convinced about her decision – seeing how he got along with her oldest friend and others they would meet as part of the Christmas celebrations. They were also planning an event to include Peter's brother and his family, who lived in the neighbourhood.

This was to be Ama's first Christmas on her own, and she was happy to return to her apartment in time to share a Christmas video with her children.

Ama and Jennie had time to go shopping, prepare for the Christmas events to be held at Jennie's house, and for Jennie to get an update on Matt. Jennie was also happy that her friend had at least the prospect of a relationship. She knew that Ama had not been looking out for anything, especially so soon, but she was really happy that her friend was open to something new and not just depending on a new career and country to be happy.

She knew how lonely it can be sometimes. Despite having her parents, her career, and friends around, Jennie knew how it felt when everyone went home to their children and families. Travelling had been an enjoyable pastime, but as the years passed, she had found it increasingly difficult to shake off those moments when all of it was just not enough.

She hoped for more for her good friend, whatever that would involve. Matt was a good start, she thought – wherever it led.

Chapter Fifteen

Ama had insisted that she needed to be back home by afternoon on Christmas Day. It was in time to send on early Christmas greetings for her children, and she thought it was good to leave her friend to enjoy the first Christmas Day with the new love she had found so unexpectantly.

"Happy Christmas, Momma!"

Ama had just had time to reach inside her apartment and take off her coat on her way to the kitchen to get a glass of water. She turned around quickly to grab her mobile from her handbag, happy to hear her son's voice at the other end.

"Happy Christmas, Jon!" she answered happily. Her last son was wearing a Santa Claus hat with the background of a palm-lined beach. She remembered that he was spending a few days home, actually with friends, who had decided to have a reunion at their favourite beach spot.

Ama was able to hear the sounds of joviality coming from the group of young people, most of whom she had known from their years at high school. Jon was always a popular child whose laid-back but friendly manner had attracted his peers. The only thing that ruffled Jon was someone being cruel or demeaning to another, especially a more vulnerable person.

He had often been seen as a champion for the downtrodden but had also found himself in a few uncomfortable situations when the injustice was linked to something one of his teachers had done. Not unexpected from those who knew Jon well, the discomfort did not lie with him but with those who saw him transformed from the happy, smiling young person to a firm and commanding presence. Jon as Ama had been told by the teachers reporting to her over the years, had never been rude or disrespectful – just so earnest that he left them actually feeling bad and questioning themselves.

Jon did not hold a grudge and never made an enemy of anyone he met. If anyone did not appreciate his candour on those occasions, they had so far not found any space to seek revenge or even to be disgruntled, as Jon went on to embrace them in every other way possible. He also wore a slightly dimpled smile which may have also been hard to resist.

"Mama, what are you doing? It's Christmas!" Jon said, smiling at his mother. At that stage a few faces appeared in the video, calling out, *"Happy Christmas, Aunty!"* extending it into the well-known ditty:

"I want to wish you a Merry Christmas. I want to wish you... from the bottom of my hea-a-a-rt!"

Ama spent a few minutes updating Jon about her activities over the last week and her plans for the next two days of the holiday. It was always nice to talk to her son. She guessed that she worried about him the most because he was alone, with no other family. Yet Jon never seemed lonely, although he did manage to take some alone time, usually on his computer, in the gym, or on some solitary walks. He also enjoyed a good movie and watching the football games of his favourite team, with or without friends.

Being alone, he was also the most likely to check on his mother, sometimes seeking her advice or venting about inconsistencies in university life and coursework. Ama could usually expect long conversations with her last child.

The conversation today was a jovial one, and she left him after a few minutes, to go back to his friends. A few of them had to make similar calls to parents and family, and they embraced the ritual of greetings adopted for the day.

Ama knew that it would take a while longer for her to hear from her other two children. She did not want to call because families had their own approach to spending Christmas Day, and she did not want to intrude on or disrupt this. She knew that her daughter would include her at some stage in the unwrapping of gifts or breakfast, and she would hear from her elder son at any time that he would get away from the celebrations with his in-laws. She drew comfort from the fact that her son managed to reach out and make up for this at different stages. Life brought these situations, and she knew it was important that she could go along with them.

Ama ended her call with Jon without any mention of her date. This was not something she felt she had to share particularly at this early stage. Besides, it might have been a one-off event, as there had been no promises that she would even see more of Matt until the new semester began in the spring term.

Ama emitted an involuntary sigh and then could not help but laugh at herself. She laughed again, a bit more loudly, as began unpacking her small bag, putting away the clothes that she had carried only 'just in case'. Jennie had given her a spa set with a range of items that smelled really nice, taking her to exotic places in her mind.

Ama smiled again, reminding herself to stay with her two feet on the ground. Jennie's story had not helped. She decided though to make a concerted effort to focus on what she knew was real. She must keep her head on finishing her degree and then moving on to the doctoral level once she is successful and able to find a job afterwards that would provide additional income. She would be lucky to be able to pursue a career that she loved at this later stage in her life. It was not a good idea to expect any more than that. It is possible that she might end up having a couple more grandchildren. Jon was still single, no plans there but you can never tell.

Maybe this was her chance to experience the adventure part of her life, going into somewhat unknown territory and hoping for the best at the end of it all.

Chapter Sixteen

Ama's mobile started ringing just as she reached her door. Instead of answering it immediately, she quickly removed her keys from her pocket, opening the door to get inside.

"Hello," Ama answered a bit breathlessly before reaching the couch, where she dropped her handbag.

It was two days after Christmas, and Ama had decided that she would enjoy the last few days enjoying the freedom of not having to account to anyone for the next few days.

She would return to course material in a couple of days after the New Year and just before the semester begins. That left her with at least a week. She had gotten up with the idea of walking to the lake that was about a mile away from the housing complex.

She packed a little picnic and a novel, deciding to take the bus for a short ride to help her find her way. It had been pointed out to her previously and she had always planned to go there at some point.

"Ama, it's Matt!" The familiar voice came across sound cheerful and firm.

"Hi, Matt," Ama responded, the breathlessness from her brief dash indoors replaced by a momentary loss of air from a completely different source. She had not expected this, having successfully removed any hope from her

thoughts.

"How are you? Did you have a good Christmas?"

"I am well," Ama answered. *"Christmas was very pleasant, though different. What about you?"*

"Well, it was the usual for me. Not quite the occasion it was in earlier years, but still with the coming together with a few family members."

There was a momentary pause before they both started speaking at the same time.

Ama really was not sure what she was about to say – maybe something about talking with her son or visiting her friend. She was happy for Matt to follow up on his unexpected call, encouraging him to go first.

"I have been thinking about meeting up with you before the semester starts... wasn't sure though how you would feel about that..." He paused, waiting for her response.

Ama smiled at the phone, not realising that she had not spoken. *"Ama?"*

"I would love that!" she answered quickly.

"Okay, that's great." She heard the cheerfulness return to Matt's tone. *"I am not the best at telephone conversations myself. Can we meet somewhere? Maybe somewhere a bit further away from the campus area, I think."*

"That should be a nice change for me," Ama answered.

"I can pick you up at your apartment. Is it okay if it's a day trip? I have an idea that would be a nice setting for us to get to know each other a little better... tomorrow

maybe, or the day after, if that's too soon," Matt ended.

Ama wondered whether she should be too enthusiastic, putting it off until the day after tomorrow but then decided that she would trust her instincts. She did not want to spend the next day overthinking an outing with Matt. Best to get it over with, right?

"Tomorrow is fine with me," Ama said.

Matt and Ama ended their call with an agreement on a nine a.m. start to their day trip. They were going to a farming community that offered facilities for visitors, including a few activities. That was all Matt said and Ama thought it was going to be a fresh experience. She loved the outdoors in weather that promised to be cool but sunny.

Ama was ready and waiting, taking a second or third look at herself in the mirror, when her buzzer sounded. She expected it to be Matt, and it was. She answered promptly, telling him she was coming down.

Matt stood a short distance from the doorway as Ama emerged, looking up with a slight smile that seemed somewhat intent on assessing Ama – not her appearance as much as her expression, her mood perhaps. He otherwise looked relaxed in grey denims and a light blue jacket opened over a cream knitted top. To him, Ama looked just as he imagined her: simply and tastefully dressed in blue jeans and a colourful jumper under her jacket. He did not pay much attention to her clothing but saw the expectant smile on her face and felt assured that this was a good idea.

Matt was looking forward to spending the day with Ama. Still not sure what he was hoping for, he was allowing his instincts to lead him. This had to be good for him. He realised that he may be testing out how good she would be with the choice of setting for their second real date. He had not done it intentionally at first but knew it could not hurt that he had chosen it... and even better, she had sounded genuinely enthusiastic about it when she accepted the invitation. This would not be the ideal setting for many women, he thought, but this was the closest to who he was and the lifestyle that best suited him. He could be wrong, but he thought it might be closer to the person Ama was, despite the dissimilar early life experiences.

Matt drove a small Land Rover, which required Ama to step up to the front seat – not an unwelcome change for someone who was considered tall by most standards for women. He had walked her to the passenger side, opened the door, and actually waited for her to be seated comfortably before closing the door. Ama smiled again at the idea of his gentlemanly ways.

This was not something Evans had maintained during the years of their marriage. He seemed to think that women expected too much – or maybe just her – that they wanted independence while still wanting the old traditional approach from men. Ama imagined that he could be about ten years older than Matt but obviously had not thought that Ama deserved such treatment or maybe this is just what happened over the years of marriage when life became just too demanding and our spouse takes on the face of the one keeping us tied down.

Matt seemed to be around Ama's age and could easily have adopted a more modern approach. But Ama shook her head from imagining this to be perfect or Matt to be more than he is. She did not even know him – not really. Ama had personally longed for some pampering, though she had been encouraged by the people she had known to think that this was not realistic for a woman of her years and experience.

Over the years, Ama had not developed female friendships. She did not feel inspired by the common stories of neglectful husbands that seemed to be the norm. She was also not much of the typical homemaker/housewife with an insatiable interest in keeping up with the most modern home décor or even in shopping generally. She and Evans had a few couples they had kept up with socially to some extent, mostly linked to community groups, but they had been otherwise preoccupied with their own family and close relatives. Theirs had been a bit of a sheltered life that Ama thought was also good for the children. Truth be told, she had found socialising with other women a somewhat dull prospect and preferred to curl up with a good book whenever she had gotten a chance. That had allowed her to escape for a while to the far-off places she dreamed about.

In any case, Ama had enjoyed seeing the world a bit through her children's eyes and involved herself in planning daily and holiday activities outside of school for many years until they seemed to be all grown up, at first, just needing lifts to meet up with friends, until they were driving or went off to university, then marriage.

During the intervening years, Ama had tried to invest

in her marriage and to take up a few hobbies. She had done some freelance writing for a local newspaper and had some interesting interviews with local and foreign activists. She had even made a few trips not too far from home, where she met people with similar interests. She saw her and Evans drifting further apart and time together became an empty experience with apparently no shared interests, nothing to talk about. Evans did not seem to have any interest in the things she liked to talk about. He had created a world of his own that did not involve her even though it might not have been intentional. Maybe the children being grown up had meant that his job was done. It could have meant time for them to enjoy together if they had been the match of her dreams, but it was increasingly obvious that they were worlds apart.

As Ama settled into the comfortable seat with Matt at the wheel of the well-kept vehicle, she determinedly shook off the reverie of her old life. She felt that this was going to be a day to remember for a long time.

Chapter Seventeen

"I hope you are comfortable," Matt said, smiling as he took his glance away from the road for a second, "because we have a long drive ahead of us."

"Yes, thank you. I am actually looking forward to the long drive. I really enjoy going out of the city."

"I do remember you saying that you enjoyed the countryside, or at least green spaces, mountains, and water nearby," he said with a grin. "I thought that this would be an ideal place, so we will see."

"You remembered that." Ama was pleased, thinking of an item now being off her imaginary list of inspiring traits. "I am sure it will be."

Matt had the car radio turned on, so there was some background music – it was classical music. Ama herself had often chosen to leave her car radio on classical music for solitary drives to work. She changed it whenever she felt the need for more popular genres that encouraged her to sing along.

The conversation between the two flowed easily, starting with their choice of music, then onto other topics e.g. love of green spaces, work, career, travel, and hobbies commenting briefly on little titbits from what they were seeing as they drove along. Ama had never really come through this area before. She had been mostly on trains when leaving the campus and its immediate surroundings of shopping areas and residential communities going to visit with Jennie. That had not allowed her to see much. The journey led them through the city before going onto a motorway that thankfully only lasted about fifteen minutes before they took on a more scenic route.

Ama had always enjoyed the countryside and remembered her own home community as a child, with rolling hills and having to pass across a stream to climb steps leading to her own home. Her father had valued their first family home that he had planned and built alongside his friend, who was a builder. She remembered how they had built up over the years, improving with all the amenities that were available. Ama had been born in that house and remembered long vacation days playing by the river, collecting small fishes. She enjoyed trips up the mountain where her father had created a garden of food crops, something that he enjoyed throughout her childhood until they had finally moved to a home that did not allow such pastimes. She nonetheless had always entertained the dream of open fields, mountains, rivers, and the ocean.

"You are lost in thought," said Matt with a sidelong glance at Ama. "I know it's a long way…"

"It's lovely," she responded immediately. "A place of dreams for me, really."

"Well, I am happy to hear that. We are almost there."

As Ama looked to the right, she was able to see the open corral of horses in the distance and in less than five minutes buildings started to appear. Nothing like the tall concrete structures of the city, these were wooden structures like small chalets scattered over low-lying hills. Lining the street, they drove along were some buildings she was able to identify as shops, a supermarket, the post office, and a pharmacy – all that you will expect in a small town. The structures were pretty and all of wood. They crossed a bridge, and looking down, Ama saw the open river, a lot bigger than the stream of her childhood. Matt kept up with some titbits of information about the town, telling Ama about the waterfall and the small reservoir that protected the town's water supply.

"Is this your town?" Ama asked Matt.

"Never been here before," he answered with a brief sidelong glance at her. She sensed that he was excited.

"I thought it would be nice to discover it with you."

Ama looked at Matt and then at her surroundings. She did not know what to say about that. She felt a mixture of emotions that she could not quite identify. Above all, she recognised a feeling of anticipation. Something new was happening, and she had no way of knowing where this new path would lead. Should she allow herself to be excited? Should she be afraid? What would the old Ama do? Ama acknowledged then that she had taken a different path that started with her decision to walk away from her previous life. She had made a first and second step in trying to create a new life for herself. Well, this is it – she was on the way.

The young girl who had married so many years ago had not been afraid. She had felt the innocence and sense of invincibility that came so easily to the young. The life she had encountered had been a learning experience that Ama had not imagined. What had she really expected all those years ago, that all her dreams would be realised? She had not really thought beyond the first step.

Was this Ama any more wise or knowledgeable? Too often she did not feel that she was. She had only gathered years of experience. She still did not know what her next step would bring and how it would change her life. The only question was had she lost her courage or was she still ready to embrace what was to come.

"I would like to discover it with you too," she answered simply, and then laughter came. She was just going to live this day fully, letting go of old anxieties, the baggage often carried by the not-so-young.

Matt looked at her with some surprise before joining in her laughter. It was an immediate bonding, at least for this one day in their lives.

Chapter Eighteen

Ama had not paid much attention to the satnav which was a built-in feature of the vehicle Matt drove and that had guided him to this place. She had rarely travelled in cars since she came, using mostly buses and trains. When she had visited Jennie, she had done some driving but had not used this device in the city that was familiar to her.

Matt asked her then if she was hungry and suggested that they find a place to eat. He had not planned every detail of their trip, leaving most of it up to how they both felt when they arrived. As expected in a small town, there were not many choices, and Ama was not really a fussy eater, happy to enjoy mostly anything that she did not have to cook herself. Making a choice, however, was somewhat difficult. She would often spend long minutes looking over a menu at a restaurant, ending up choosing something that was familiar or something that did not live up to what she expected. That, however, rarely stopped her from eating it.

Ama had had breakfast before leaving and felt that a drink would suffice until lunchtime. Matt had packed a small cooler, and they each had a drink after driving out of the town centre to park at a spot that was a little above ground in the sloping hills. They came out and stood at the fences that separated the roadway from the grassy slopes, looking out at the homes, farmland of animals and crops.

It was still early in the day, so most people would have been occupied with their jobs. The town they had left behind a few minutes earlier had not had a lot of traffic, with relatively few vehicles in comparison with what the busy urban setting offered, parked or moving along. There were signs of families with small children and a few older ones, and Ama remembered that it was still the holiday period when schools would be closed.

Matt and Ama drank water from small bottles, saying little as they enjoyed their surroundings, which were pleasant and invigorating in the crisp winter air. The sunshine had held up so far with no sign of this changing in the blueness of the sky. This ensured that the temperature also was more than manageable for a day out, especially for this time of year. They expected the weather to be colder in the coming months between January and March, so it was good to enjoy these milder days while they lasted. It could change at any time. In this rural community, it was likely that the winters would be harsher than the city; perhaps they might have snow. Ama had never experienced snow and instead imagined how beautiful this place would be in the spring into summer months, with the greenery in full bloom.

Matt had contact with a vet in the area whom he had met at a conference a few years ago. They had actually attended the same veterinary school a year or two apart but had not known each other. Matt told Ama about that as he explained how he had chosen to come to this place in particular. It was the closest to the city campus where Ama lived and where he now had a similar flat. Ama also learnt that Matt spent very little time there, escaping whenever he could. He had started the programme only in the autumn and often needed to be away, which she had assumed was due to family commitments.

This friend, Tony, ran a veterinary clinic in the area and had invited Matt to visit a number of times in the last six years or so while Matt had managed his own practice miles away. Things were changing for Matt, but he remembered this as a place that he could share with Jennie. It so far looked just as Tony had described over the years. The two men had not talked so much directly since they met, but they had exchanged intermittent emails mostly related to their work. The fraternity was small, especially for vets who worked in more rural communities, and having contact with each other had helped in keeping up with the most modern practices. Having access to information and updates via journals and professional websites was generally not enough. Matt's career had started to undergo a significant diversion, but this was still in its very early stage. He was still in the process of working it out. Maybe sharing some of this with Ama would also help, he thought.

Matt told Ama about Tony, asking what she thought about meeting him first before they went off to enjoy their own adventure. He had also thought that Tony would have some tips for activities or places they could enjoy. There had not been any real information about what was available to visitors. It was obviously not a place that was set up to attract tourists. Matt thought that was okay and hoped it would be the same for Ama.

Ama was happy to join Matt in becoming reacquainted with his colleague and friend. He had a number for him and called immediately to tell him that he was in town and was able to drop by. Tony was surprised and happy to see Matt and the friend who had come with him.

The day had been a lot more than Ama had expected. After meeting Tony, who had seemed a friendly and laid-back professional who enjoyed his work, they enjoyed a short tour around his small veterinary clinic that involved two members of staff, a receptionist and an assistant. Tony felt that he might take on a partner, another vet to share the work that could increase at times, but he was not sure how sustainable that would be in leaner months. Tony had pointed them to some of the activities that might be enjoyable for Matt and Ama, including a place they could enjoy their picnic closest to a lake as well as horseback riding. Both were Ama's choices and Matt felt pleased that she was able to identify things that she would like to do. She had really wanted to visit a farm as well, and they managed to squeeze in a visit to a farm run by a family. She realised that this was all familiar territory for Matt and really appreciated that he was willing to spend the day sharing all of this with her.

The evening had ended with Ama's first time on a horse. She had always had a dream of this and had missed a few opportunities that had come up over the years at home. It was all that she had imagined after she had got past her nervousness about being so close up to such a large animal and high up when she was eventually able to get on with Matt's help. Having him close by with encouragement helped her to feel better, distracting her also with funny stories of his early riding days with his siblings and friends.

Matt himself looked really magnificent on a horse, leaving her feeling slightly in awe of getting closer to him. For so many reasons, it was a memorable experience that she could now tick off her bucket list.

Matt and Ama left the town just before the sun disappeared completely over the horizon. The journey back seemed too short, as they both shared the feeling of not wanting to end the day just yet. When they arrived back in the city, they had agreed to have a quiet dinner at a small pub Ama had never visited, just a few minutes from her home.

The day seemed to have brought them somewhat closer together – the feeling that comes from sharing an experience. Although Matt had spent most of his life in a community not so different from this one, having Ama with him and helping her to experience something so unique for her brought him a lot of joy. He was feeling that they had a real memory, which brought some sense of hope of what could be in the future. After so many challenges in the last years of his life, having to raise his two children with all that it involved without his wife, he felt ready to open his life and heart to new possibilities.

For Ama's part, she felt that even meeting Matt and then spending this day together was more than she could even hope for after the last two years that she had faced almost on her own. Looking back on her own life she had not expected the turn that it had taken. She had never planned on walking away from the marriage that had occupied her entire adult life, having married at an age when most young people were enjoying the freedom of early adulthood with all that it involved. Going out with a man was a really new experience and more so being treated with such respect and kindness, having someone who was literally opening doors for her. Could she dare hope?

Matt had a sense of humour that had shown itself often in the day they had enjoyed together and Ama was laughing when he parked the vehicle and was quickly at the passenger side to help her out. She looked up at him seeing his own smile as he reached out for her hand and closed the door behind her. She felt his hand closing around hers with a sensation that passed through her chest and went to her knees. It was not overpowering but enough for her to acknowledge.

Matt did not let go of Ama's hand as they walked into the pub. He acknowledged that he liked the feel of it. Ama was not a small woman, reaching not so far from his own 6'2" stature. She was slim but firmly built with long slender fingers that fitted well in his hand. He looked at her to see how she felt about him continuing to hold her hand. They had held hands briefly during the day as it was often needed as he supported Ama over less even terrain or other activity. This holding of hands was not the same. He liked it and as their eyes connected, he had the sense that she did as well. This for some reason brought him a deep feeling of satisfaction and he felt again the slight spark of life growing in himself.

This evening, both Ama and Matt felt the need to ask questions of the other – questions they had not previously felt confident to ask, mainly about life experiences and relationships that had brought them to this moment. Ama shared a bit about her broken marriage and her children, while Matt talked about the challenges around the death of his wife, which left him not only without a mate but as a single parent with the responsibility of two children, with all the challenges this involved including special needs.

Matt's son had been diagnosed with autism not long after his wife had died. It had increasingly become obvious that the behaviour they had tried to come to terms with in Alan was more than just a few quirky traits. He was identified early with a high intellectual ability, speaking, remembering, and sharing information related to a specific interest in animals – far beyond what Matt would have been able to teach him. He had a unique way of playing and had never seemed comfortable going out or generally interacting with others, particularly other children. At a children's gathering, he would stay close to the parent who was present and would usually be anxious to leave.

Going into nursery from three years old appeared like a nightmare for Alan and this did not improve when he had to transition to the primary school. Raising Alan had been more demanding than Matt was willing to acknowledge at that stage to Ama. He had accepted it as his life. His daughter, Marie, had seemed fine – a lot like her mother – and clung more to Matt after her mother's death. She had always been a gentle child making friends easily and being always a good girl and sister to her older brother, who demanded a lot of time and patience. Transition to high school seemed to have been more than she could manage and she noticeably became more timid and eventually was not speaking away from home.

Staff, including a psychologist working with students, quickly identified Selective Mutism. There had been many days when Marie would complain about being sick and did not want to go to school. She spoke to Matt and close family and very little to a few close friends she had known from early childhood but was otherwise silent with others. There was a lot of concern being raised about Marie's well-being during those years, which was often quite daunting. There had been some consideration of autism but this was not the case.

Having studied Psychology and been involved with children with special needs, Ama was well aware of the impact this had on families and understood more about Matt's journey. His children were both young adults now, with Alan only recently talking to his father about the possibility of marriage to a young woman he had known from high school. His interest had shifted over the years from animals to people, and he had gravitated to neurosurgery, doing very well in this profession.

Marie had been able to move out from the home she had shared with her father, going off to a college a few counties away, sharing with other young women and finally choosing a career in Art and Photography. She worked at a well-established Art Gallery in the city not far from where she had studied and was happy in a community of friends she had gathered over the years. She had enjoyed travelling initially with her father, taking pictures in lesser-known places. Marie had had small showings at the Art Gallery where she had worked. She also liked blogging in which she shared photographs along with ideas about the places she visited and the people she had met.

Matt had learned a lot from his children's development in order to be the parent they needed. This had taken him in different directions, including looking at ways to incorporate his early practice in veterinary science into Psychology and Psychotherapy. He had accessed the growing body of research on the impact animal care and being around animals had on children with social-emotional needs and social communication disorders.

Ama felt even more drawn to Matt as she listened to his story, feeling inspired by the steps he had taken in being a good parent and his ability to adapt and allow the challenges he experienced to lead him in a whole new direction. She wished then that she could use her own experiences in a similar way.

Chapter Nineteen

Ama barely heard her alarm, letting it ring on as she laid on her bed, lost in her early morning reflections and not yet willing to break this initial stage of her morning routine. Today was going to be the first day back from the Christmas break, and Ama was mostly looking forward to getting on with her programme. She was happy with the career she had chosen and embraced all that she was learning, anxious for it to lead her into the practice she hoped to establish. There was a lot to think about.

Ama also thought about Matt, fully aware that he was almost always on her mind. They had not met since the day they had spent together, and Ama continued to savour that memory along with the chats they had on the telephone since then. Matt had been busy with his own veterinary practice, which she now realised included the work he had developed hosting children and families with special needs. He had basically interwoven Psychology into his work, requiring him to keep in touch with new research and current trends. She was happy to have learnt that about him. He had actually only taken a break from this on specific holidays. When he came to university, he generally left this in the hands of very capable staff, but it still demanded regular input from him, explaining in part why he was often back there.

Matt and Ama both expressed the competing feelings of meeting up in class but being perhaps too busy to spend the time they would have liked together. They were happy, though, and excited to follow this through and to have it work out in the way it should. Ama was ready and out the door within the hour it took for her to organise herself, get dressed, and have a bit of breakfast. She felt like a child on the first day.

Ama arrived in class at the same time as the professor came through the usual back entrance. The professor was one she had had before, and who was typically a few minutes late, but this morning seemed to have made a New Year's resolution to be more on time. Ama recognised a tiny hope she had carried of meeting Matt along the way but acknowledged now that it was not his style. He had usually made an entrance arriving after everyone had settled in and the lecture had begun. There was not going to be any change from him, and she now understood why this might be so.

Matt had not travelled from his permanent home and veterinary practice over the weekend, wanting to stay there for as long as possible before the university programme took off. He had actually put off leaving to the last possible moment despite his excitement of seeing Ama again after a few days – well just four days actually but as he had driven along in the early morning fog, he acknowledged how much that overshadowed the major issue of completing his own programme in Psychotherapy. He recognised what that appeared to mean about how he already felt about her. What it did mean, he would have to reflect further.

The door to the lecture hall at the back of the class opened, and Ama felt rather than saw Matt entering. She seemed to recognise his stride and general aura. *Can that actually happen?* she mused. But in a few more seconds, he was there, moving into the row just behind her and in a diagonal position where he had a direct view of Ama and where she could see him without turning around. They shared a silent greeting when he sat down, with the unspoken agreement to focus on the lecture. This was a priority that they both accepted.

There were just two lectures that day and a group meeting. Matt had never been in Ama's group, and they considered that this arrangement may have its merit. In a brief meeting after their first lecture, they decided that they would meet at the end of the day for a catch-up, maybe early dinner. They were being sensible, not allowing their obvious attraction to impact their work. Matt had a lot of responsibilities in addition to the coursework, and Ama knew that she also needed to give a lot of focus to her learning, not having yet settled into the new systems and approach to study. She also needed to devote some time to other more personal and family matters as they might occur. She did not want to disappear from Jennie's life and needed to be there for her also in this new relationship and time of major transition.

When Matt and Ama met that afternoon, they both felt like kids in a candy store. They reflected together that this felt somewhat like a fairy tale, a bit unreal, how they were feeling about this budding relationship. There was a lot that they still did not know about each other, but it was a real surprise on how their feeling had escalated over the last three weeks – a significant jump also from the day off in the countryside.

Should they create a specific schedule for meeting during the week, or should they leave it to happen spontaneously? There was no map that they could refer to on how they should approach this situation that was so new to both of them. At that moment, they decided that they would just see when they could both take time from their busy schedule with Ama looking at the regular times when she would take a walk along the river or go to the gym or spend time looking at a movie at home, something she did on a regular basis as things she enjoyed and found relaxing. She had always had a cut off for work, insisting on having a balance of work and relaxation in her life. The time for both may not be equal, but relaxation and time out had always had a place of importance in her schedule.

Ama realised, though, that this was not quite the same for Matt who had always worked endless hours, not quite sure where work ended and personal life began. His personal life had also been filled with work-like issues, particularly around the care and development of his two children. Despite so much in common with values and dreams, the practicalities of their lives have so far been significantly different. This was something they both needed to acknowledge as they savoured the bloom of love that hovered over the present reality. They agreed to approach this with care, at a pace that matched what they needed to do in identified responsibilities and what they now wanted from this new relationship.

The semester rolled on and seemed to pass quickly

with classes that Ama was really enjoying. She found time for joining the group at the local pub on just two occasions. Matt had not been present at either of these. She learned from him that he had not attended those normally in the previous semesters and it seemed that on the occasion that he had, the real purpose had been to meet Ama. They smiled over this idea when he expressed it and Ama wondered at later times on her own whether this was actually true – that their meeting and blossoming relationship was somehow preordained. Ama nurtured her spiritual development and hoped this was part of God's blessing for her.

Matt decided that time with Ama was something that he needed to schedule into his days. Doing this was entirely new to him but needed to be done. He had not said much to Ama about this, but it became a pattern for him to call her almost every day in late evening to find out about her day, and sometimes they talked on until they both needed to sleep. It meant that, for the first time, Matt was actually focussed on some level of time management in this recent attempt to create a life for himself outside of work and family duties. They did not have such regular meeting times but took time every two weeks or so for a real date – sometimes just dinner, sometimes a walk along the river and a picnic when Matt made sure and remained in the city before having to rush home on the weekend.

It was on the last day of the semester that Matt shared his hope that Ama would be able to come with him for a visit to his home. He had spent very little time until then in Ama's own apartment, which appeared as an unspoken agreement between them.

Chapter Twenty

It was Friday evening, and Ama was on the train to visit Jennie. The semester had started a month earlier, and they had barely had a chance to talk to each other. She realised she missed having Jennie available to talk over important issues. Even before she had come abroad, they had managed to keep up talking at least every week since Ama and Evans had finally been separated. Life had definitely taken on a happier tone both for her and Jennie, and they both agreed that it would be really good for both of them to spend some time together.

Ama had heard more about Jennie's almost-fiancé, now referred to as 'Pete' and had shared snippets of their budding relationship with Matt. She really needed this time with her friend just to ensure that she is on ground level. It was so easy to get lost in the clouds, that dreamy space where she thought this new relationship might belong.

Ama planned to stay for most of the weekend, feeling that she was caught up with assignments – a good place to take a break. Matt was also off on a conference until Sunday, when Ama will return home in time to do some quick preparations for the week. Her girl-time with Jennie was overdue, she thought, as she neared her stop, looking forward to it. Pete had decided to take some time for his brother and his family to give Jennie time to catch up with Ama.

Pete and Jennie had been almost inseparable over the last months since they had met and both agreed that a weekend without seeing each other was not such a bad idea after all. They had already exchanged keys to each other's homes. Well, Pete had a key to Jennie's home, with him being in the temporary accommodations he had rented after he met her, moving out of the B & B where he had initially stayed for his family visit. He had actually extended his stay recently, not ready to put thousands of miles between himself and Jennie just yet. He was thinking of staying long enough to be there while she got her affairs in order being leaving the country. There were a lot of decisions to be made, particularly on Jennie's side, but they were also still in the getting-to-know stage in their relationship, despite their early commitment to a life together.

Ama's taxi had just stopped when she saw Jennie coming through her front door. Her friend had obviously been looking out for her, as anxious as Ama was for them to catch up with each other. It was a cold day, and she just grabbed hold of Ama's bag, hustling them through the front door before their usual hug in greeting. Jennie seemed as happy as she did the last time Ama had seen her over the holidays, but she also seemed to carry an aura of calm that her friend was pleased to see.

Ama knew her friend had been concerned about her life since her parents' death, reaching a stage when she was not sure what was next, waiting to step out on the next phase of her life. She now seemed to have accepted that this was it. She had a plan that she was happy with, an unexpected but more than pleasant one.

The two friends sat curled up on the couch in Jennie's living room, sipping a cup of tea. They had put off their plans to go out until later in the day or maybe the next day before Ama had to leave. Talking over some of Jennie's plans seemed more important to both of them.

Jennie needed some reassurance from her friend that she was not acting hastily but mostly seemed determined that this was the right course of action for her. She did not think that everything would be settled at home before she left, knowing that she would have to return, maybe more than once for her to complete the transition to a new country. Jennie did not think there was any urgency and was leaning towards renting out her home for the first few years at least. She and Pete had talked it over and felt that it would be a good idea to have some space available, as they both had family ties in the country.

Ama was not looking forward to losing her friend when she herself had only just migrated, and was hoping that they would be able to get together more frequently than had been the case where Ama had lived abroad. Jennie and Pete had not set any dates for getting married not seeing it as a priority. The first step was for Jennie to meet the rest of the family in Pete's home. She was considering the idea of continuing to teach as well, but all of that will be worked out once she has taken the first step.

Jennie also heard about how Ama's relationship with Matt was progressing, recognising it as going at a completely different pace but noting definite signs of progress, particularly with Matt's latest invitation for her to visit his home. The friends were both happy to be together at this time in their lives. Ama had admitted that it was not easy to talk to anyone else about this, particularly not her children – not even Jon at this stage. It was all so new for her. It was not something that she could slip into any conversation with any of her children. At this stage, she was almost happy not to have to tell her own parents about this.

Ama would not have known how she would talk to her parents about anything that had happened over the last two years. Ama's father had always said that she would always have a home with them but she was sure that he had not considered the breakup of her marriage to Evans. The marriage may not have met their early approval, but they had fully accepted their son-in-law over the years and had him in that position for life. For moments in time, she reflected on the scene that would have been created if they were still alive.

Andrew had called during the Christmas holidays, and she had been happy to talk briefly with him and mostly listen to her two- and a half-year-old grandson, telling her about his toys.

She had also spoken to her daughter Susan and granddaughter as they celebrated their family Christmas. Ama and Susan did not talk as much as they used to, but Ama felt she needed to give her time to get used to the idea of her parents not being together and living within an easy distance of regular visits.

Ama knew this had been hard for Susan, but she felt

that her husband was very supportive, and with a big family, Susan was fully embraced. Susan had also been her father's little girl, between the two sons with whom he had not fully connected in the latter part of their lives. They had challenged him as his daughter did not, and maybe as men usually would. Evans did not handle this well, liking to be the man of the house, the one who they would always look up to. Ama had never been sure how to handle this herself.

Ama had not grown up with brothers, and she and her father had always been closest among her two sisters including the eldest who was quite a few years older than her and had lived abroad for years. She had returned home briefly after her university graduation but had then decided to take up residence in a country she had grown to love. The age difference had not helped Ama and her sister to have a close relationship, particularly in a family that had not been very open or affectionate. Ama had written to her a lot in her teenage years but had finally accepted relationships in her family while longing to create something more in her own. It had seemed better with her younger sister for a few years, but over the years, they had grown further apart, each with their own responsibilities. Her little sister did not do well when attention was not on her and seemed to become more competitive in the way she and her family related to Ama and hers. She had one son and a daughter. Her older sister and her husband had a son who had grown up not really knowing his cousins despite a few visits home in the early stages. Ama remembered them visiting when he was about five years old, and the next time she had seen him was at his grandparents' funeral.

Ama reflected on all of this after a day spent with Jennie. They had certainly talked a lot, finding it easier to stay at home as the weather into the evening turned colder with the rain falling. They had ordered dinner, as both decided that they were not really in the cooking mood and not having gone to the shops. It was fun hanging out together, and there was a lot of laughter as they recalled incidents as far back as their own school days, bringing up names of people they had not seen or spoken to for years.

At one point, the two friends had also filled the house with music that they both enjoyed, singing and dancing to tunes they both liked. Ama thought it would have been easy to fall asleep after that, but instead, thoughts had shifted to her own family. This was often not a topic she enjoyed dwelling on. She prayed for a more fulfilling future for herself as well as her children in their new families.

It was quite late when she heard her phone ringing and saw it was Matt calling. This was much later than usual, and she had not expected to hear from him. His first day at the conference would also have been busy.

"Hi," answered Ama.

"Hi, back," Matt answered. *"I thought of you and couldn't help calling. I wasn't sure you would still be up though."*

"I have been lying here, just thinking. I'm glad I didn't fall asleep now..." Ama said.

The conversation was not a long one but ended up being just what Ama needed to finally fall asleep.

Chapter Twenty-one

The days were longer, with rainy days replacing the endless weeks of winter frost that was particularly evident in the early mornings. Ama was intrigued by the combination of sunshine appearing even on the chillier days. She had grown to love the feeling of sunshine on her face and brightening up what was otherwise the greyest of skies. She would usually dress warmly, as she had been advised, learning how to address the temperatures that were still too low for her. It was fun to be dressed in a way that she had only previously seen on television. The downside was that dressing continued to take much more time than it did at home. Home seemed so far away, another world. She had no plans to visit, mainly more sensibly due to time and cost, but deep down, she did not feel it was the right time for her.

She woke up one morning, during the early days in April, to one of those bright days evident through her bedroom window, ready to take the short walk to the university. She felt happy with how things were going and was looking forward to seeing Matt's home.

Looking around her, she realised that the trees were once more covered with green. Had this happened overnight? She gazed around in wonder at the scene – trees that had been brown and bare, with sticks for branches, now had fresh leaves. It was beautiful to see this transformation.

Flowers had started to appear before this, which she heard heralded the coming of spring. She remembered writing a poem about Easter and new life for a school assignment and felt that this was exactly what happened: 'a time when all things were new, plants, trees, and flowers too'. She smiled at her musings, surprised that she remembered this after so many years. Ama started to believe that all things were possible in this atmosphere of miracles.

Jennie had left two weeks previously for the start of what would be her new life, while Ama started to look forward to entering the second year of her programme. There was still a lot to do before that happened, including a few exams which stood in the way. She was hopeful of success, but the prospect was always a bit daunting. Ama had not been able to help the tears from flowing with her best friend leaving, but they had had time to prepare for it and would be seeing each other again soon – first when Jennie returned in a few months, and certainly with Ama's visit to them in the not-too-distant future. It was a promise made, and one Ama definitely planned to keep.

Everyone in Ama's class had started to talk about their next steps with the end of the programme happening for many of them. Ama and her classmates had started at different times, so she would have a few months added. She prepared herself for a lot of change when most of the people she knew would have left. She had started thinking more seriously about the path she would be taking towards her own career. With the end of the semester happening in a week's time, she was prepared for a meeting with her academic and professional tutor, which she had to book in that day.

Matt had not been able to get away last weekend, and Ama had spent most of her time working on an individual project and doing some cleaning of her flat as well. She had been doing only the most obvious things over the semester and sometimes did not feel she was up to the extensive cleaning that she felt was currently needed. She was normally good at getting the basic household chores done, and not having anyone else contributing to any disarray did mean there was less to do daily or whenever she chose. Anyway, she had been putting off what she called her spring cleaning and had managed to get a start over the weekend. It was not really a big job, as the flat was quite small and relatively uncluttered.

Ama had enjoyed her usual walk along the riverbank, stopping for tea at one of the cafes, which were usually quite crowded during the weekend. This was a really pleasant atmosphere, and Ama had usually walked past. She felt in awe of herself for her decision to stop that day, not intimidated by the people who seemed to fit in more than she did, enjoying an afternoon out with friends and family members. Being alone on occasions like this was often quite difficult, but she told herself this was something to which she must adjust.

Ama was really not usually afraid of being on her own. She had always been one to choose her own company over being lost and even alone in a crowd. This had meant that she did not feel excited to just go along with people when there was no real connection with them or when she was not prepared to engage in an activity that was too far off from what she could tolerate. She found that she was finding it increasingly difficult to keep up small talk just to drown out the silence and was left often with conflicting feelings whenever she was forced to do this.

While Ama had always been relatively popular, particularly during high school, there had always been a limit on how far she would go to maintain friendships. Everyone around her seemed to have accepted that while at school. As adults, people may have been less accepting of her tendency to turn down invitations for drinks or for some popular event. She had had the excuse of family and more children than most of her friends or colleagues.

Ama had rarely shared how important she had felt it was to remain close to her children and also that she really enjoyed spending time with them. She had always made it her mission to find events and activities they could enjoy together. She had spent money all year long on games that they could also play at home. These games often provided a background for discussion, either during or afterward.

Ama accepted that she was still adjusting to being a single middle-aged adult as well as being in a new and bigger country, but she mostly enjoyed the anonymity, not having demands from friends for a while. She was happy for the opportunity to get on track in creating a life for herself, other dreams deferred. University life kept her busy, like having a job would, and she was usually happy to have downtime just for herself, reading, looking at television, or walking by the river, joining her university mates about twice during the semester at the pub.

And now there was Matt. He was still somewhat in the background and not yet something she could factor into her future. Despite the regular phone calls and meetings, they were really still in the getting-to-know-you stage. Without any real conversation about it, they both seemed to accept that this was sensibly longer for more mature adults who had had almost a lifetime of experiences with a lot that would continue to go on alongside any new relationship. This was a thoroughly unplanned and happy time that they savoured. Maybe there was some contradiction in this, but there was no rush.

Ama's meeting with her tutor happened on the day the semester officially ended and the day before she was due to join Matt at his farm. He was coming to meet her for an early start the Saturday morning. He had been at the campus that week for a few closing sessions, so they had spoken quite a bit, meeting face-to-face for dinner as well, also joining their mates for a drink one evening before he and Ama had gone to a late movie. They had both expressed a preference for the theatre but had not yet been able to plan for this. The evening rolled out with a lot of spontaneity that fitted well into the spring atmosphere when everyone was happy to be outside again, saying adieu to the cold, cloudy days and dark evenings.

Matt had given Ama an idea of what to expect. She had even used a map to work out the direction they would be travelling to go to his farm/veterinary clinic, sounding increasingly like a well-being centre.

Ama awoke slowly to the crisp morning air with signs of the brightness that had been promised for that day and the rest of the weekend she had agreed to spend on the farm. She had gotten used to giving a lot of attention to the weather, which had not been something she would do at all in the home she had known from childhood. At home, it was either sunny or rainy with clouds that gathered mostly before it would rain. Cloudy days were rarely seen otherwise, and you had an idea of how much rain would be falling based on the time of year, but this warranted very little attention, particularly as there was only minimal change in temperature.

Ama sometimes missed the warmth and casualness attached to the weather she was used to but was generally able to accept the constant change in weather conditions here in her current setting. Checking her phone for weather forecasts or temperature readings was a part of her daily routine, mostly to guide her on choice of clothing.

Getting ready here certainly took more time, she mused, as she maintained the use of tights under her jeans while slipping on a pair of socks under her ankle-length boots. She also wore a vest under her jumper that was not as thick as what she had worn over the winter months but ensured she was okay in the cool air. She decided that it was prudent to take a light jacket with her, knowing that she felt cold much more quickly than most people. The clothing she chose was comfortably casual for a day out, she thought.

Ama had packed a small overnight case the night before with little more than a single change of clothing.

She always chose to have an additional outfit for any unexpected event. Matt had not outlined any itinerary when she had agreed that it would be more practical for her to spend the weekend rather than ending a day prematurely with so much driving for Matt in one day. He had promised that his house had adequate rooms available for guests, particularly with his children no longer there. They had always accommodated friends and family visiting in a simple but spacious setting. He thought that she would like it and was looking forward to hosting her and giving her a glimpse of his home as well as the work that occupied so much of his time and attention.

Matt arrived promptly, actually a few minutes before the planned eight a.m. start of their journey. They were travelling to the southeast of this large island, a place known for its lovely greenery and farmlands known as the garden of all the counties. Ama had heard a lot about it and was looking forward to a first-hand experience. The drive without stopping would take them just over two hours, but Matt had promised that they could have a stop along the way if Ama wanted. He accepted that her first time on such a long journey might be a bit tiring and was being sensitive to that, but Ama knew that he would normally undertake this journey without stops and did not want to force a stop that was not necessary. Matt had had to convince her that driving with her was different and he was prepared to see it on this occasion also through her eyes. He had smiled as he said it, giving her a deliberate compliment about her eyes, saying that they were beautiful and expressive. The conversation had taken a different turn after that.

Matt was able to flirt and was often full of compliments, with what Ama could only describe as a soulful stare while he did. She may have read a bit too many romance novels! She admitted to finding him almost too handsome to be interested in her, and maybe it was this thought that resulted in Ama feeling shy like a school girl. She was also not quite used to these personal compliments up close anyway after being married for the greater part of her life up until then. The shyness was quite embarrassing for her in the beginning. She was a grown woman, after all, she insisted to herself. But the truth was that having the passing compliments from strange men or colleagues to whom she was not attracted was quite different from receiving one from Matt. She liked him and he liked her. This was so new, and she was gradually surprising herself with signs of growing confidence, initiating a compliment of her own or reaching out to hold his hand as they walked along the river.

Signs of the growing affection between Matt and Ama had not gone further than a kiss on the cheek or on the forehead, which Matt often did. They would more often hug each other in hello or goodbyes, with his form of greeting starting after a few dates, having become a standard form of greeting since their trip to the nearby countryside during the winter. Ama found herself feeling very conflicted about any change at this point. She was definitely not in a rush for any increase in intimacy between them. She did not think that this was going to change over this weekend, and this had been indicated with their choice of pace and Matt's assurance of a room having been prepared for Ama at the farmhouse. Matt had a housekeeper that had been with him for years, during the period since he became a single father. He had not thought of this at first, but he had eventually accepted that maintaining the large house and taking care of his children, particularly with their additional needs, had been too much.

Matt's neighbours, sympathetic to his situation, had almost insisted, and one of their widowed relatives had been recruited. She and Matt had hit it off almost from the beginning with her down to earth manner and quick wit, she had also been good with the children. She had bonded well with them accepting them as they were, following the guidelines that Matt shared mixed with some of her own and they had grown attached to her. She had nowhere else to live after they had grown up and eventually moved away, and there were lots still to do in Matt's home. She was also going down in age herself, and Matt tried to limit the demands he made on her, almost against her will. She liked having people in the house, apparently missing the children with the demands that had previously filled her days.

Matt had said a little to Ama about Martha, and she was happy to have someone else in the house. In so many ways, Ama still felt married or at least not quite single and perhaps too invested in being a mother to three grown children. She did not think that they were ready to have tangible evidence of her moving on from their father. She felt that Matt would have gotten that message from all the conversations they had had over the few months. She was not sure she was even ready to talk about a relationship that included sexual intimacy. She was trusting that it would happen when it needed to.

Matt's greeting to Ama was especially enthusiastic that morning. The hug felt warm and inviting and told her how much he was looking forward to the time with her. Ama herself felt the warmth of her growing affection for him reaching to the surface and welcomed him in reciprocating the greeting. They both expressed joy about the good weather too, which Ama was able to identify as a lead topic of conversations between people here. She laughed at the evidence that the reputation they had on this issue was well-founded.

Matt helped Ama into the vehicle, putting her overnight case on the back seat, and they were off on their weekend's adventure!

Chapter Twenty-two

Matt and Ama were both laughing at their almost simultaneous response to the sight of a man on a bicycle, dressed in a bird-like costume with bright yellow feathers. He was obviously celebrating the spring, but the look of him struggling to balance himself in the cumbersome and likely overweight costume encouraged a humorous response. Ama had never thought of herself as having a sense of humour. She tended to analyse a joke to such an extent that she often missed the point, which had often caused her to be the butt of the next joke among friends. But she did enjoy laughter, and was doing a lot of it with Matt. At these times, she felt almost like a different person. She had rarely appreciated Evans attempt at humour which often seemed more like sarcasm, so this was a new experience. It was laughter filled with a *joie de vivre*.

The miles passed by and despite the speed of the car, it did not seem like Matt was going too fast. Ama guessed that the wide lanes of the motor way accommodated the seventy miles per hour and more sometimes. The surrounding environment was not very picturesque for a while with signs and tall green trees blocking any signs of life in the towns and villages. Ama hoped that at some point she would be able to see some of those towns but did not feel bored as she and Matt engaged in a range of conversations some about the history of some of the places they passed. Matt seemed quite knowledgeable to her, prompting more questions from Ama initially connected to some of the names on the signs. Today was a field trip and she was enjoying every minute.

After about an hour of driving, Matt took a turn off the motorway without saying anything to Ama. She looked at him questioningly wondering if something was wrong. He looked at her but said nothing as he drove into a tree-lined lane and entered an open area with a petrol station and stop shop near the entrance a minute later. He took another turn past this and further inside was the unexpected burst of life seemed to appear out of nowhere, people, families with children were leaving their cars, moving towards what looked like a fairy tale like castle in the background. It was actually a mall filled mostly with cafes and restaurants and just a couple utility and clothing stores, an amusement park. Matt had decided that Ama would prefer to stop for a slight change of scenery before continuing their journey.

Ama was pleased that he had shown such consideration, although she had been fine so far. They had had bottles of water and fruit, and that had been enough for her. But she expressed her appreciation for his thoughtfulness, exchanging smiles as they agreed to sit for a while. Matt explained that the mall was partly linked to the town a couple of miles away from the motorway but it was expected also to cater for motorists, particularly those with children and other people needing a rest.

The rest of the journey took them another forty-five

minutes of motorway before took the turn into a more town-like environment, with another twenty miles to go through the outlying streets as they avoided the expectedly busier town centres. The journey at this stage took them through open spaces of forest on both sides, farmland, and narrower streets before wide open roads again.

On the final stretch, they drove through narrow lanes where Matt had to stop at times, pulling aside to accommodate one or two persons on horseback. At other times, he also had to pull aside into spaces to let oncoming traffic pass by. This went on for about thirty minutes before they came to the town that was Matt's home.

Ama recognised the sign with some anticipation. Although they had been talking a bit along the way, there had been an atmosphere of stillness, broken mostly by Ama asking about something she had seen with brief comments from Matt. She was looking forward to seeing Matt in his element and felt almost tangibly that he was having similar thoughts, wondering how she would like this major chunk of his world.

"Dr Matt! You're home!"

A young boy rushed to the vehicle as they drove up. It seems that he had been looking out for 'Dr Matt' and was happy to see him. Matt waved to the boy, who may have been between ten and twelve years old, cautioning him to stand aside safely. Matt looked then at Ama, confirming that yes, this was home. He seemed to watch for Ama's first response before jumping out and coming to the other side to open the door for her. He never failed to do that, and Ama had begun to get used to it.

"So, here it is finally," Matt said, "What do you think?"

Ama did not really know now what she had expected, but this first view of Matt's home was a beauty from first sight. It was at the end of the last lane they had taken, which Ama realised then was actually their driveway, as no other houses were seen at the sides of what she could only describe as a grand building in the shadow of rolling slopes in the background. It was as much greenery as she could hope for, with a faraway view of horses and other animals grazing on either side, along with a few barn-like structures. What could she say about all of this?

"Wow," she finally emitted.

"It's really beautiful, Matt! So much more than I expected…"

With a laugh, Matt took her hand, introducing her to David, the little boy who was trying to find anything that needed to be taken inside for Dr Matt. Matt explained that he would normally bring David and the two other children who lived on the compound some treats. David's parents lived in accommodations that were provided for the foreman and his family. He was the oldest, with two younger siblings.

"Good morning, Miss Ama," David answered politely, with a glimpse of dimples punctuating his gleeful smile.

"Dr Matt, can I help you? You have something for me to carry?" he spoke to Matt in childlike impatience, anxious to get things going. It was always more fun when Dr Matt was around.

Matt turned around briefly, telling David that he could take out the large brown bag in the back seat. He did not stop walking with purpose towards the front door of the mansion. How was it that Ama had never thought of Matt's home in this way? She had considered Matt's parents to be humble farmers. How did it get to this? She could not wait to hear and see everything.

This was going to be an experience of a lifetime for her, she thought. What else did Matt not share about his life? She had questions but decided that she would not be anxious and just wait for things to unfold and for Matt to share what and when he was ready.

Matt pulled open the great oak door for them to enter into what was a huge hallway of high ceilings, wide large potted plants and almost life-sized ornaments on either side. The area was partly carpeted in brown mixed with colours that reflected the muted colours of the wall and the wide majestic staircases on both sides. Who was Matt? Some kind of royalty, she wondered, feeling increasingly less sure of herself and why she was here.

The outside of the building had not prepared her for this, and she had not been in many of the houses she had seen since arriving in this new country. Ama had really only seen Jennie's home. All the houses she had found tended to look alike, and she realised that maybe she did not really know what they looked like inside. Jennie's home was not elaborate and looked like many of the family houses that she had seen on television. It was well-maintained and had some beautiful pieces of furniture and fixtures that she had associated with living in more developed countries abroad. She had gotten used to visiting Jennie's house, which was not so different from a middle-class home in her country with a few additions. Matt's home was very different, even with just this initial view.

Ama looked at Matt questioningly, just as a short roundly-built woman came through one of the doors at the end of the wide corridor, walking quickly to greet Matt. Ama guessed as soon as she saw her that this was Martha, who at least looked almost exactly as Ama imagined her. Her eyes sparkled with pleasure and kindness as she greeted Matt and then Ama, her smile of welcome all that Ama needed to feel comfortable. Matt had not let go of Ama's hand, maybe recognising that she needed some reassurance that she was indeed welcome and how much he wanted her to be here.

Ama decided that she would relax and enjoy the rest of the weekend in this lovely place. She was happy to be here with Matt and to get to know more about him.

Chapter Twenty-three

The day had been remarkable, and Ama still had to pinch herself to believe that she was actually in this place. She had not really been able to imagine Matt's home, and the closest to it might had been the village farm they had visited in the autumn. She guessed that it was really not so different. What made the difference, though, were the rolling hills stretching out behind the great mansion – which she still called it. Matt had laughed at that term. To him, it was not really that big or grand. These buildings were actually not uncommon around the city and in the countryside in particular, but to Ama, they were places where rich people lived, people like royalty.

There had been so much to do that Ama had not had time to share her own news with Matt from her meeting with her professional tutor and advisor. That could wait, she thought, deciding to talk to him about it the next day. She would be happy for his input in making a decision, as she did not have much knowledge of what was available to her living here.

Today had been about learning about Matt's world, and it had been a busy day between his direct work in the Veterinary clinic – which on Saturdays was open from eleven a.m. to two p.m. It would open earlier when Matt was not at the university. Matt had only had time for a sandwich, which Martha had had prepared for him. Although he had encouraged Ama to stay and have something more before joining him, she had declined, not wanting to miss seeing him at work.

Matt was comfortable in his element, but then he had always intrigued her with that air of confidence, though lacking in any arrogance or cockiness. He liked what he did, and it was at the forefront of his manner as he interacted with his clients who brought in their smaller animals. He was the only veterinarian for miles and, therefore, there was also a lot to do. When he closed at two p.m., he was off – with Ama tagging along – to visit two farms where he dealt with some issues with larger farm animals.

At the clinic, Matt had been assisted by a young man just out of college who was interested in becoming a vet. The young man had recently replaced Matt's previous assistant, who had gone off to veterinary school after a few years working at the clinic. He was introduced as Antonio (mostly called Tony). Though new to the job, Tony appeared to be quite an efficient assistant. Matt explained, during their drive to the nearby farms, that Tony had been hanging around the clinic for years throughout school. He loved animals and needed to work and save for university. He longed for a scholarship but was not going to be fully dependent on getting one.

The afternoons at the farm/clinic were devoted to families, mostly with children coming for a horseback riding lesson or time in the petting zoo. A horseback riding lesson or experience was accommodated by David's father, Jackson, or Matt himself when he was free. Ama learned that this was not so much about learning how to ride as spending time with animals and enjoying the open spaces. The children were all having some type of social and emotional difficulty and had been referred by the local GP, with whom Matt had developed a relationship going back to caring for his own children. This was part of the new venture that Matt was in the process of developing, which explained his quest for psychology/psychotherapy qualifications.

Children who did not ride spent time playing with farm animals, including the two dogs who roamed happily in as well as outdoors. They had been outdoors for a run following David's father when Ama had arrived, so had not been there to greet her. Large and beautiful white and brown sheepdogs, they were full of energy and would usually greet guests with sloppy friendliness. Ama had been introduced to them – *Sherlock* and *Hardy, named* after two well-known literary characters – when she returned to the house after the farm visits with Matt. They were not allowed in the clinic to avoid any clashes with the other, less rambunctious animals who had been brought in for treatment, vaccines, or maintenance of general care so they had not yet seen Matt for the day.

Matt's eventual meeting with these household pets was one to behold, and Ama could not tell which of the animal species was more excited. She could not restrain the laughter that came naturally while looking at Matt interact with these two beautiful animals just before they were introduced to her. Sherlock and Hardy seemed to accept her as one of the family and were eventually drawn away with the offer of a treat. Matt explained that, despite their size, they were less than a year old and spoiled as the only dogs on the farm since their mother had died a few months earlier. They were definitely not there for work, but many of the children visiting also loved spending time with them.

Although Sherlock and Hardy had their calmer moments, a few more anxious and shy children visiting preferred petting the smaller, more docile animals, like the family of rabbits. There were also two goats, two ponies, and some ducks that the children fed scraps of bread at the edges of a pond. A couple of them fully grown were truly majestic animals. There were about five children with a possible age range of five to ten years old, there that afternoon, each with a parent who chatted with Matt and each other as they stood aside, keeping an eye on their children.

Intermittently, a child would call out for their parent's intervention, but the animals mostly attracted all their attention. The three older ones had ridden around the fenced areas stretching about a quarter-mile from the main house. The house occupied by Jackson and his family was in the outer area beyond the fencing which allowed some sense of their own home environment while also allowing a presence on the huge land space that was part of the property. A wide stream flowed just behind this cottage, flowing from the hills that might have been a few metres beyond this, visible from the entry. She was looking forward to seeing all of this the next day.

The visit by the children and their parents did not last too long, and after about two hours, they were left free to enjoy the evening. It was dusk by six p.m., and Ama opted for a quiet hour sitting on the back porch, enjoying some time alone before being joined by Matt. He had met with Martha to catch up with the week's events and work out any details for Ama's time with them. Ama had chosen to lie on the hammock that occupied space just off the porch and under a beautiful sprawling tree with low branches. She felt at peace in this place, falling into a gentle doze just as Matt appeared.

Matt looked relaxed despite the busy day he had had, first driving for more than two hours and then with all the activities at the farm itself. Ama wondered how he still managed to look fresh and at ease.

Matt tried to stop Ama as she sought to pull herself out of the hammock. "You don't need to get up," he said jovially. "You looked so peaceful lying there. I did not want to disturb you."

"No, it's fine," Ama responded with a chuckle. "I do not want to fall asleep. I want to hear everything about this lovely place and don't want to miss anything."

Matt reached out a hand to help her up to a sitting position, and Ama chose to move across with him to one of the lounging chairs on the balcony. The sun was sinking fast in the distance behind the range of mountains by this time and they sat together just absorbing the view together along with the increasing coolness of the evening. The temperature had dropped considerably, but Ama did not want to distract from the moment by getting the coat she had left in her room.

As though reading her mind, Matt reached for a blanket folded on a shelf behind them and draped it around Ama's shoulders. What had made him such a thoughtful man, she wondered again. She was having difficulty accepting him as an actual part of her life. Was she making more than she should of these acts of generosity and attention to her?

Their eyes met for one instant, and Ama felt flooded with a rush of emotions that she imagined again to be reflected on Matt's face before he drew her attention once more to the fading sunlight. Colours that flashed across the sky in a few short moments before it was all gone. They remained seated in silence as the darkness descended. At some point in their hushed conversation, Matt had reached across and held Ama's hand. She never wanted to let go.

Ama had thought that they would have an early evening after the long, busy day, particularly for Matt, but was still anxious to hear as much as she could about him and this place he called home. Matt told her that Martha was preparing a special meal for them, which turned out to be quite a feast with music playing in the background. The house felt empty except for them as they sat at a six-seater table set just for two placed in an area off the family living room area.

Matt told her then that this was the family quarters where he and the children had mostly occupied. There were larger rooms to the front that were used when they had guests, usually Matt's siblings and his nieces and nephews, and intermittently friends of Matt and the two children also accommodating their parents whenever possible. He had so far had a full life raising his children taking him in a different direction from what he and Sarah had initially planned. As he looked at Ama, he realised that there might be much more to come, letting her know that he was looking forward to what the future could hold.

The meal had been delicious and was accompanied by exchanges about the day's activities and a few tentative statements, mostly based on Ama's obvious interest in how all of this had developed. Matt seemed comfortable as he provided the missing information over a glass of wine as they sat together in the living room. The room had such a cosy feel of family. He had brought her here to introduce her to this full version of how he lived and some of his hopes for the future. Without any commitments, Matt was telling Ama that he was seeing her as being part of this in some way. Ama was intrigued with feelings of excitement as well as anxiety about this, not quite certain about what she could bring to this already extraordinary life that he enjoyed.

Matt ended up filling in all the missing strands of the story of his life and how he had come to own this beautiful property with life on this farm. Matt and his wife, Sarah, had been living a couple miles from this home, close to the farm owned and run by his parents. As a vet, Matt had been building his practice in this predominantly farming area, continuing to help his aging parents and the local gentry, which included this farm owned by an elderly couple. As a young boy, he had spent a lot of time there working alongside their old vet and had gotten close to a couple of distant relatives of aristocratic family scattered across the country. They had liked Matt and had encouraged him to pursue his love and interest in veterinary medicine, seeing him as being an exceptionally bright young man. Ama drew this from his story, in which Matt seemed to downplay the couple's thinking about him, treating him like the son they never had.

Matt and Sarah had been married for about nine years with their second child, a daughter, when the couple died within about two months of the other after a lifetime together. By that time, Matt had been their vet for about five years after the death of the vet who had served them for more than thirty years. The husband had gone first, leaving his wife, who had been ailing before this. She had not been in the frame of mind and body to tell Matt anything, and it was not until she died that Matt was called in by one of their attorneys, who announced that they had left the only thing they had owned – the property with this mansion – to him.

There had been no money left for them to be able to maintain this inheritance, with the little, there was having been left for their remaining help who had cared for them. In their will, they had encouraged Matt to sell off a few portraits they had put away and some of the land that could help to fund renovations. They had had some awareness of Matt's dreams from conversations he had had with them over the years and had expressed their happiness that they could assist in him realising his ambitions.

For months, Matt and his wife had contemplated how they would manage this inheritance and make the transition that was needed, but finally, they had, renting their own modest property for a reasonable sum and moving into the old mansion without any renovations. They had managed to obtain a good price for two acres of the property. This helped them to start the much-needed renovations that had been overlooked by the old couple, but they agreed to move slowly otherwise towards their goal. After all the years of dreaming, Matt recognised the possibilities that were then spread out for him and for his wife, who had loved her career as a teacher. The saddest part of the story was that the anniversary of their moving in coincided with Sarah's first symptoms of the cancer that would take her life in two short years. Matt had been left to grieve and build this place on his own while learning how to care for two small children.

Without a word from Matt, Ama began to have a clearer picture of what the last years of Matt's life had involved. She was being introduced to what he had created from dreams, ambition, love, and dedication, and she wished in her heart for an opportunity to contribute to the rest of this story, if just for the present, learning about the path that Matt had been travelling on this journey. They were able to celebrate Ama's presence with a glass of wine and some dancing, which was a good way to end the evening. Matt had promised Ama a full tour of the property after a much-needed night's rest.

Matt and Ama shared a warm embrace as he left her at her bedroom door. She felt the emotion of the moment stirred up further from the more poignant details of Matt's story. Since his wife's death, Matt had not had any woman in his life in the way he was drawing Ama in. Female friends who had been close to the family may have had some of the attention they were seeking, but Matt had been mostly grateful to the people who had supported him over the years, particularly with his children. He had had no time or any real inclination for romance. This was a turning point in his life, and he wanted Ama to understand what this meant for him and what it could mean for her if and when she was ready.

Both Matt and Ama knew there would be a time to express and talk about those feelings and what this meant, as they both felt the pull of their undeniable attraction to each other. They also knew that it was so much more than a physical event. There was so much more to talk about, to find out, to understand as they moved forward. Tomorrow was another day, and they were both looking forward to their time together – perhaps the start of a new phase in their lives.

Chapter Twenty-four

The brilliant rays of sunshine burst through the open space in the thick drapery of her bedroom, drawing Ama out of her slumbers to embrace the day ahead of her. If her dreams had not been enough, she was reminded of where she was almost before her eyes were opened to the sunlight. She smelt it in the air and felt it in the softness of her sheet. She was in a place of beauty, reflected in the bedroom she had been given – a lovely shade of cream with curtains in bronze and green. A fluffy cream rug surrounded the canopied double bed, high above the floor. She had only seen a room like this in the movies and imagined from descriptions in the novels she had enjoyed.

Ama realised that some of the furnishings had been enhanced from the previous owners of the property. It must have cost a lot to refurbish them, but Matt had said that a lot of the cost had been absorbed by the sale of some items, mostly to antique shops in the city area. A few had also been donated to the town's museum, developed by a local historian and his group of enthusiasts. Matt had indicated that not all the rooms were like hers; especially the children's that were more modern and quite simple in décor. He had correctly thought Ama would appreciate the historical setting of the one she was given.

Except for the outer architecture, most of the building

had been redone into a more modern structure over the years, which, according to Matt, was more practical in terms of the cost of renovations and maintenance. Besides, he was not really a big enough fan to try to maintain these reminders of past eras. However, he did work on keeping the structure in honour of the couple who had made all of this possible. The sale of a large parcel of land had been needed for the major structural projects.

Ama's room was ensuite, and she completed her normal routine, getting dressed with some excitement for the day ahead. Dressed in her casual outfit in readiness for the activities of that day, Ama restrained herself from skipping down the stairs to meet Matt for breakfast at the appointed hour. She was actually about fifteen minutes early when she reached the bottom of the staircase leading to the dining area where they had dined the evening before. Matt was not there but she heard voices further towards the back, following them to find Matt and Martha along with Jackson talking together, the dogs lying down quietly with heads nodding as though following the conversation and waiting their turn for attention. They all stopped as Ama's footsteps warned them of her entrance. turning around to greet her with enthusiasm, Matt moving toward her at the doorway with his brisk stride to hug and welcome her.

This was really nice, Ama thought, smiling at them and at him. She loved him, she admitted in some shock, the idea and emotion of it exploding in her mind. I love him. *I love Matt,* her mind spoke so loudly that she looked at him in some joy with some panic as she wondered for one moment if she had actually spoken out loud. Of course, she had not, she told herself in relief as Matt drew her into a brief exchange with his workers, mostly about the day he had planned – a tour, horseback riding. They would begin after breakfast. Ama knew that she would have a lot of time to think about those feelings, how real they were and what it could mean for her future. Of course, that would also involve Matt's own and so much more.

Breakfast was a larger meal than Ama's usual fare of fruity cereal and sandwich to go. It involved eggs, bacon, mushrooms, beans, hash browns, with the option of toast, fruits, and yoghurt, juice, and tea or coffee. She had previously been exposed to such a breakfast only on overnight stays while on holiday or for work events. She was not usually a big eater but seemed to enjoy it much more when she did not have to prepare it all. And she did that morning, as she looked forward to the day with Matt. She was prepared for a late evening drive back home, with Matt planning to stay in the city for a couple of days himself. The clinic would be managed by Matt's assistant, as it usually was on his days away. The weekends were the busiest days, starting from Friday, when Matt liked to be present.

The day was her second day on a horse, and she was at ease with Matt at her side. He kept the turns short – not more than fifteen minutes or so at first – to give Ama time to get used to riding, and in between, they walked through different spots that he thought Ama would enjoy. They eventually had a picnic at the side of the river that ran through the farm, Matt opening a bag that Ama had not really paid attention to, hanging at the side of his saddle. It contained fruit, cheese, ham, and turkey sandwiches, cake, and two bottles of the fruity beer that Ama usually enjoyed at the pub.

It was a treat that accompanied them as they sat and enjoyed being together, sharing openly about past experiences, and talking about childhood experiences in such different circumstances while seeing so many similarities in their lives with parents who seemed to have had it all worked out.

Matt and Ama shared more current information about their own children and what and how they were doing along with their own high points of joy and moments of disappointment. They talked about their plans and hopes to put their pending qualifications to good use. In between this, they held hands, stared together at the mountains, water, and sky, and walked through the stream with their shoes off and pants drawn up to their knees.

At one point, Matt pulled out a small canoe that was moored in a cove under some trees hanging over the water, and they rowed out in the small lake just for the fun of it. Some funny stories of childhood, teenage years, and the years raising their children – vulnerable and foolish moments – made them laugh and feel so closer to each other. Their laughter rang out at times, with Ama splashing water on Matt, resulting in more wetting than they had planned. It was a good thing that the sun had stayed out, making it one of the warmest spring days.

Ama found time to talk about her university advisor's suggestion that she take up the opportunity to pursue her doctorate immediately as an extension of the master's programme. It would take only an additional year being added on to her current programme, with most of the time being used for a placement when she would also be working on a thesis. Matt's own programme was coming to an end just about the same time as Ama's original master's, and he was happy to think that there was good reason for her to stay on past the original time. He felt that it was coinciding with some of his own hopes.

Ama was concerned about finding a placement where she could also earn some money to add to her dwindling resources, and Matt was right there to offer her a placement at the formal opening of his Well-being Clinic for children and adolescents. He saw this as a role for Ama, as he would not be able to manage it all. He was planning to look out for a new assistant when his current one went off to vet school, but he knew that a new person would still mean he was the only qualified vet in the clinic, leaving him with less time for the Well-being Clinic he wanted to formalise. This was driven by his own experience as well as the love he had seen in his late wife's work with children, which had extended far beyond the teaching job she had been paid to do. He saw some of the same devotion to the job in Ama, along with her drive to make a real difference wherever she went.

Before Ama left that day, the decision was made. They knew that they had yet to reveal their feelings for each other.

Chapter Twenty-five

Matt and Ama left the farm just before dusk that evening for the long drive back to the city. It had been a full but relaxing day, and they had talked so much about almost everything. It was understandable then that the journey was completed mostly in silence. There were a few glances at the times when light flooded the car just long enough for them to see each other's face – serene and expectant glances reflecting their happiness in that moment, but obviously mulling over all that the last forty-eight hours could mean for their relationship. Darkness had descended, appearing to give them space to be alone in their thoughts while still being together, with an intermittent touch of hands as Matt removed his from the steering wheel. The drive was perfect and just what was needed, Ama thought.

They both felt reluctant to leave each other as Matt stood at the main door of Ama's apartment building. He had helped her with her overnight bag and a few home-baked goodies that Martha had insisted she should have. She had prepared a really great feast for their day out so that there had been a lot remaining. She seemed ready to be a mother to Ama, as she had been to Matt's children and Matt himself over the years. She commented more than once on Ama's slim build wondering whether she had been eating enough being so busy and missing home. She seemed to like mothering in the few hours Ama had been there and looked forward to seeing Ama again soon.

Ama and Matt stood facing each other, the two bags leaning against the wall near the door. She felt the full force of his presence as he looked down slightly seeming to examine every contour of her face. Ama felt lost in his eyes, which held a kind but passionate glaze. They had a clear view of each other in the bright light of the courtyard that came when anyone was there. It did not seem like a moment to be shared in public view, but neither seemed to have any thought of that. In any case, the place was much quieter than usual, with the end of the semester and many students having gone off to some sort of vacation. It was also Sunday evening which was usually quiet time with few people outdoors.

By mutual consent, Ama and Matt leaned into the other, Matt having to bend his head to accommodate the two inches or so that he was taller than Ama. Ama raised her head and then their lips met. There was an immediate shock or feeling of sparkled awareness, before the kiss deepened into one of extreme passion and longing. They had never kissed like this before and they stopped for a brief moment to look at each other before the kiss resumed with even greater intensity. It seemed to go on forever before they both had to stop, coming up for air perhaps.

"I love you, Ama," Matt spoke quietly and simply after taking a few moments to catch his breath, moments in which his glance had never left Ama's face. Ama for her part did not seem able to recover from a kiss that she had never had before, after so many years of marriage. She stared back at Matt, no words coming to her.

"Ama, I know this may be unexpected for you, but I have been carrying around this awareness for months, I think. From the moment I met you, I felt something that had been dormant in me for a long time. I know you have had a difficult time over the last two years with the breakup of your marriage, and do not want to rush you into anything. I know you have a lot to consider. I believe that you share some of those feelings, but that it might be soon for you." He stopped for a moment, bearing a slight but maybe a bit nervous smile, his look never moving from Ama's as their glances remained locked.

"I love you, Ama," he repeated, before his arms closed around her again, this time in a more gentle than passionate embrace, one that Ama leaned into with gratitude as well as the deepest affection. She felt and recognised that but was hesitant to name it otherwise. She did not quite recognise what those emotions meant and did not want to make a mistake. She felt a mixture of fear with the exhilaration that lingered after that kiss with Matt. She found it hard to believe that this beautiful man was declaring his love for her. Everything she had experienced until now spun around in her mind. She was finding it hard to turn off those thoughts. She held on to Matt instead, not saying a word.

Matt seemed to understand and gave Ama those moments, remaining silent. They did not seem to keep track of how long they stood there hugging each other before the sudden awareness of someone coming through the door, drew them apart. As the couple walked past, Ama had some time to change focus, which was helpful. She had needed that moment.

Ama's hands remained linked in Matt. That seemed so easy and natural to them. She smiled broadly as they looked at each other.

"I think that I love you too, Matt," she said finally. "But my feelings seem still so locked up with past experiences and what that means. So much still to consider, you know."

She searched his face for the understanding that she believed somehow would be there. It was what she had seen in him, and that gave her so much comfort. She believed she may truly love him but needed time... she needed more clarity somehow, she thought.

Matt, for his part, realised that Ama was only recently single and had an ex-husband as well as children, though adults, in the background. The latter, and maybe even the former, may not yet have come to terms with her walking away after nearly thirty years. He knew she was looking for more understanding from her two older ones and particularly her daughter, who had always shared a close bond with her father and was initially angry with her mother, who she had thought was the one who had initiated the decision to seek a divorce and break up their family. From what Ama had told him, she had not seemed to recognise that she had had her own family to focus on for at least five years previously. He felt Ama would be considering all of this as well as her loss of confidence after what she saw as a failure. He was prepared to give her time and would let her know that he would be here, waiting for her to be ready.

When Matt responded, Ama was not disappointed.

"I understand, Ama," he said. "I just needed to tell you. We still have a lot to work out." He returned her smile, accentuating the cleft in his chin that she found somehow so attractive. She giggled softly.

Matt looked at her questioningly.

"I feel like a schoolgirl, I'm thinking," she answered, causing Matt to emit a laugh himself.

"Let's make some plans then, after a good night's rest and reflection," Matt suggested, to which Ama immediately agreed. Matt had planned to stay over a couple of days with Ama before returning to the farm. The clinic was on a slower schedule to give Matt time for personal and family activities. His assistant would be there to manage any situations that could not wait for his return to the practice the following week. Then they would both be off on a short vacation, with Matt going off to visit his children. Meanwhile, he and Ama had a few decisions to make, professional as well as personal ones, after their declaration.

Matt and Ama hugged each other closely with Matt ending the embrace with a profound kiss on her brow. They smiled as they reluctantly disentangled from each other, their linked hands the last just before Ama took hold of her bags, with Matt opening the door for her to proceed into the building. She went ahead for a few moments before looking back, almost at the same time as Matt started walking away while looking back to see her go up the stairs. Another brief wave before Ama disappeared up the staircase, lifting her small suitcase up the short staircase to the first floor, where her apartment was located.

Ama took out the key to open the door to the flat, entering just to lean against the closed door, emitting a long sigh – contentment, joy, confusion, fear – an amalgamation of different feelings that she needed to unpick. She decided on an early bedtime after a glass of milk. She eventually thought to include a warm bath, which she usually found to be relaxing.

Ama realised that she had a lot to think about before she could fall asleep. Part of her mind pushed for her to take this in the best way. Matt loved her, and she loved him. That was the best situation possible, so what was there to be anxious about? Everything, that challenging voice of her mind could not be silenced. Everything, in the form of children and ex-husband. Was she prepared to deal with all of this? Was she prepared to manage a relationship at this stage in her life? Was she ready to move forward with her life in such a big way? How was she going to handle all of this? She needed to thread carefully and work it all out. In any case, she had known Matt for less than a year. How sure was she of the love they had both professed?

Chapter Twenty-six

Ama had remarkably fallen asleep not long after snuggling under the covers of her single bed. She had done much of her worrying while in the bath, and by the time she had sat at her counter drinking a tall glass of milk, she had been all worried out, her mind making room for the joy of the moment when this beautiful man had professed his love for her. Unremarkably, she thought, she also loved him. Everything was better than she could have imagined. Those thoughts had accompanied her to bed as her mind dwelled on the weekend they had enjoyed together as well as highlights of the months they had known each other.

Everything will work out, the optimistic Ama thought. God was in charge of what happened next, she prayed which would have been moments before she had fallen asleep.

Ama was just about to go downstairs when she heard her bell ring. She knew it was Matt and skipped down the stairs to meet him at the door. She was as happy to see him as he looked, and after a gentle embrace, they walked off together, heading for a little café on the riverside to begin their day together.

"Are you hungry?" Matt asked. "I feel starved, so I'm going to have a big breakfast," he announced. This usually involved toast and hash browns with eggs, slabs of bacon, other meats, beans, mushrooms, and whatever else was on offer, including cheeses and pastries.

Ama did feel hungry but, as usual, had difficulty making decisions about what she was going to eat, so decided to follow Matt, adding to some of his choices rather than ordering a full meal on her own. She started her meal with a glass of water and fruit with oatmeal and ended with a cup of hot chocolate, one of her favourite drinks. Matt shared in the fruit and went straight into his meal, ending with a cup of tea.

They chatted lightly, Ama sharing her thinking about the farm and the weekend they had enjoyed, and planning for the day to talk about their future. Ama talked about her need for an internship, with Matt encouraging her to do it at his Farm/Well-being Clinic. They both felt that it fitted well together, but they needed to work out the timings for this given the distance between Matt's home and the university. The general thinking was that it should be done weekly at first – e.g., a week at university and a week at the farm – and then for a more extended period of practice which would suit the university's expectation. In the end, Ama would have a year added to her course before producing her final doctoral thesis. This was something she would welcome as the ultimate achievement in pursuit of her career.

Matt expressed his confidence in her and how happy he felt that he could be part of that. They both thought that it was amazing how their careers merged together, with Matt having had the vision of merging Psychotherapy, with his work as a veterinary surgeon. He insisted that he owed it all to all the practitioners who had been so supportive as he struggled to manage the needs of his children. They had opened up the field of Psychology to him, and he was full of gratitude for the direction it had taken him, including now the meeting with Ama. This was not anything he could have foreseen.

Matt and Ama spent most of their time on the river before taking a train into another part of the city, where they did some sightseeing, mostly for Ama's benefit. Matt realised, too, that it had been a long time since he had engaged in these activities, including museums and art galleries. They rested intermittently, sitting for tea in an open picnic area where their talking over different events continued. They also had moments of silence as they dozed on the grass, cosily in a corner with some distance between themselves and other couples and families also enjoying the spring day of sunshine.

Matt and Ama decided to end the day with dinner at a place where there was a live band, where they were able to dance together for the first time. It was a fitting end to a day when, even with people all around them they had felt in their own world, created by the growing signs of deep friendship as well as passionate love for each other.

They talked also about their children, mulling over what would be the best time to introduce the other, initially just the mention of having met someone they valued as part of their future. There was no date for that. They had time, and in Ama's case, that time was especially needed.

They decided that enjoying this new life just between them was the current priority. The rest will fall in place at the right time.

Chapter Twenty-seven

Ama had slept well waking long after the sun had risen on the horizon. She was feeling hopeful about the future with herself pursuing the career she had always wanted – now alongside Matt – in the immediate future and with a new, unexpected relationship with a man who seemed to have so many of the qualities she had only dreamed about. After their day together, talking out some of the immediate plans for working together and building a relationship wherever that leads them, she had gone to bed feeling a lot more secure and happier than she could have imagined for herself, particularly after the last few years of her marriage and after the divorce.

It seemed later than she planned, she thought, quickly reaching for her mobile phone on her bedside table, anxious to see the time. She and Matt only had a half day together before he was leaving to return home and to prepare for his trip to spend time with his daughter and his son, who did not live far from each other. She and Matt planned to meet for breakfast at nine a.m. It was just minutes before eight o'clock, she acknowledged with relief – just before the phone rang. Matt, she smiled to herself.

"Mummy! You need to come home!" It was her daughter, Susan, and it sounded like she was crying.

"Drew and Amelia have been in an accident. They are both in hospital. Drew is in surgery for internal injuries, and the doctors are not sure if he will survive..." She was speaking quickly, almost hysterical. Ama knew how Susan found it difficult to manage situations when she was not in control. She may often see things much worse than they are. She told herself this after her initial panic, choosing to work on helping Susan to calm down so she could understand what was happening.

"Susan, where are you? Are you at the hospital?" Ama asked calmly. She heard Susan trying to hold back her tears and trying to answer

"No, I'm at home," she answered between some hiccups. *"Dad called me from the hospital. He's there. I'm at home with the children... They had left Adrian with me as well. We had him for the weekend... to give Drew (using her pet's name for her brother more than anything expressed her fear) and Amelia some time together... you know..."*

Ama sighed. It was just like Evans to pass on such news to Susan. He always had trouble managing difficult times, and now he had Susan losing her mind with worry. Ama did not ask then about Amelia, hoping that no news was a good thing.

"Okay, Susan, try not to worry," Ama told her. *"I will call your father to find out. You just pray that Drew will be okay, as he has been in the past. I will call you back."*

Ama spoke soothingly but firmly, trying to relieve Susan of all the worry she had taken on. Susan had always been the sister looking out for her brothers and trying to ensure everything worked as it should. In a way, she drew her role from her mother's, being in charge of making sure everything worked. She had in this also been more of a perfectionist than her mother. Ama's approach was more to ensure she did her best so that things were good enough. She managed her anxiety and always hoped that Susan would reach the place where she accepted not being able to control everything.

Ama called Matt to let him know that she may be running a bit late and immediately called Evans' phone.

"Evans, Susan just called me. What's happening with Andrew and Amelia?" she spoke briskly.

"Hello, Ama, he was in an accident. The car's a write-off, I'm told..."

Evans was rambling giving Ama information that she did not consider relevant.

"How is he? Is he out of surgery? And how is Amelia," she spoke clearly.

"Amelia is fine – she was not hurt. Andrew just came out of surgery. The doctor said the surgery to stop internal bleeding was successful, but he is still critical. They will be monitoring him over the next twenty-four hours. He is not awake," he provided the information Ama needed in even tones.

"Are they worried about his survival?" Ama felt she needed to ask that question, praying the answer would be positive. She refused to give herself permission to worry; otherwise, she would not be able to cope. She kept praying and reminding herself that Andrew had always managed in the past to get out of scrapes – like the time when he and

his friends went diving off cliff during a trip to the seaside with some friends, deciding to celebrate their final A-level examination. She had not heard of this dangerous event until long after.

One of the boys had suffered a minor injury that could have been a lot worse. Then there had been the accident when his vehicle was hit by another car, smashing in the passenger side, allowing Andrew to walk away without a scratch. Even as a child he had liked to jump, falling and getting up without a bother. She prayed that this would be another of those times. She waited almost breathlessly for Evans's response.

"They report that the damage was not as bad as they initially thought, but they are waiting for him to wake up. It depends a lot on how his body reacted to the trauma."

"OK. Andrew is a fighter…" Ama ended the call with Evans without any further conversation.

She called Susan immediately, assuring her that Drew was out of surgery and encouraging her to continue praying for his recovery. She reminded Susan of how tough her big brother Drew had always been. Susan had had a lot of experience attending to Drew when he brushed aside the fuss she made.

Susan seemed a lot better when Ama hung up the phone. They were both still worried, and Ama had to decide on her next step. Would she need to go home to help with Andrew's recuperation? Amelia did not have any serious injuries but had been sedated because of her heightened emotional state while still at the hospital for monitoring. Ama would call back later when she was likely to be awake. It was too early in the morning there – five hours behind Ama's time. She got ready and left her apartment to meet Matt at their breakfast spot, still mulling over her next step and praying for Andrew's recovery.

"What's wrong?" Matt asked Ama, as even before she sat down, he was able to tell that she was worried about something.

Matt had woken early, not used to sleeping late from life on a farm, and had left his apartment for a leisurely walk to the café where he would be meeting Ama. He was thinking about how quickly she had become so important to him. He was even feeling reluctant to leave her after they had spent almost every waking hour of the last four days together. They just had a few hours before he would have to leave her and he was looking forward to seeing his children and catching up with their news, but realised that he was already missing Ama just thinking about her not being with him.

Matt was also wondering if it was a good time to tell his children that he had met someone. He had mentioned meeting an international student on his course and talking to his children about travelling somewhere far in the summer, but he had not spoken about her as someone he liked or spent time with. Maybe the next few days would be a good time to do this. Both his children were adjusting well to adult living even while sharing in a supportive community, and they had close relationships.

Matt now thought they would be ready, especially after talking about their father being on his own in that big house. He felt sure that they would like Ama and that she would be good with them. He had only hesitated because he had not been sure about their future together before these last few days. He felt sure about them now, though. Whatever form that relationship takes, they had one. He felt happy that they loved each other.

Matt had only a brief moment of worry that it had something to do with him, and he quickly dismissed it almost at the same time. Had something happened at home?

"What happened, Ama?" Matt asked.

"My son, Andrew, and his wife have been in an accident," Ama announced as she sat down. "He is in the hospital." Ama felt tearful suddenly as she responded to Matt's full attention of concern.

"How is he? Do you need to go home?" he asked. "I can come with you." Matt made up his mind quickly, not feeling comfortable about Ama taking a nine-hour journey alone while being worried about her son. He did not feel that he could let her leave so soon after they had declared their love for each other. He also did not want to acknowledge the idea that he was, to some small extent, afraid that he would not see her again. That would be foolish, he told himself.

Matt looked closely at Ama and realised that she was holding in her own fear for her eldest child. She was trying not to break down. Putting aside his own concerns, Matt closed in on Ama, wrapping his arms tightly around her. Feeling her totally collapsing into his embrace and receiving him with her own arms holding onto him and pressing her face into his shoulders, Matt knew that she was not running away from the newly found love that they now shared. He was not going to lose Ama, whether he went home with her now or at some later date in the future.

At that moment, as Ama felt herself sinking into Matt's embrace, she received the powerful reality of this man. She felt strongly that God had led her to this man, and a deep sense of gratitude and love swept through her. As she held onto him, she felt that here was finally someone she could depend on. This moment somehow convinced her that Matt was able to receive her strength as well as her times of weakness when her knees were buckling. Ama felt suddenly less afraid – less afraid for Andrew. She felt convinced of God's Presence at this moment with her, with her family, and with Matt as a part of her future. After long moments, she felt calm, raising her head to meet Matt's query, his eyes reflecting the love and concern that she expected.

"Thank you, Matt, for being here," she said, touching his cheek lightly. "This news came so suddenly and in the middle of this unexpected joy…" Emotion still threatened to overwhelm her, but she went on, "I feel better now. Thanks, too, for offering to go home with me."

Ama talked to Matt then about Andrew and how many scrapes he had always gotten into as an active child growing up. She drew comfort from the fact that the prognosis was not as bad as they initially thought. Maybe Evans, in his own anxiety, had also blown things up in his first call to their daughter, and the surgery had gone very well. She would stand by and continue praying as she waited for Andrew to wake up. She would find out from

Evans if his doctor had been on duty and decided to get in touch with her for some more reliable news about Andrew's condition.

Dr Mason had been the family GP for a number of years, working at the public hospital alongside her private practice, and Ama had developed a close relationship with her, one that was both professional and personal as they shared news about happenings in their own lives. In some ways, they were like colleagues, as Dr Mason also respected Ama in the way she managed her personal and professional life. Dr Mason had a practice near to the school where Ama worked, and they had met when Ama was pregnant with Jon, her last child, making a shift from a previous physician.

As Matt and Ama kept vigil, waiting for news that Andrew was awake, and then to hear from Dr Mason, they talked about the visit to the place that was her home. Ama would want to go home at some point and maybe the summer would also be a good time for him to go with her. They did not have to announce a relationship, but it would be good to see Ama in this family setting. Matt loved to travel to new places and had not yet been in that part of the world that he imagined as eternally sunny with lovely beaches and tropical rain forest. He knew, of course, that it was much more than that, but still thought about these amenities as a perfect background even for the most mundane life experiences.

Ama and Matt agreed to talk more about this in the weeks ahead as they celebrated the good news that Andrew had woken up and seemed well. Ama had spoken to Dr

Mason, who said that the internal injuries had actually been minor and the surgery had been successful in mending the tear that was causing the bleed. There was no reason why he should not be fine after a couple of weeks to recuperate.

Matt's final day in the city with Ama had definitely not gone as they had expected. It was late evening before everything seemed to have settled down. They decided on dinner in Ama's tiny flat, ordering a meal as Ama had not felt much like eating for most of the day. It was Matt's first visit inside Ama's flat, and it did not feel at all strange. He had found it as expected – not much different from his own, although a bit smaller – but he saw the small stamps of Ama in the mementoes and extra bits, including a rug in which they sat, leaning against the two-seater couch.

Matt knew that Ama would be tired after the overwhelming emotions of the day and was the reason that they had chosen this option instead of going out. He found it hard to leave her though as they said goodnight. Matt had insisted on postponing his trip home, calling his children earlier to say he would be a day late. He had decided that it was the right time for Ama to meet his children and planned to introduce the idea to her the next day before he had to leave. He did not expect her to be ready to leave with him, although he wished that could have happened.

After some thought, Matt was able to accept that such a change in their plan would not be best for Marie and Alan. They could certainly set a date and event when this could happen, though. He would talk to his children together, knowing that Marie would be able to help Alan with the news. She had become so much better at managing change and seemed older or more mature than him in so many ways now despite the gap in their ages. Alan always needed some extra time to adjust, which, of course, they all understood. Over the next few days before the semester started. Ama would also have time to spend time with her family, with regular video chats.

Matt did not stay long the next day, realising that he had just needed to be there to ensure that the news of Andrew's recovery had not changed and that Ama would be okay; no sudden flight home was needed. They had had a late breakfast together with a leisurely walk along the river before he was able to leave her. He had shared his intention of telling his children about her. They had talked at some length about this, and Ama eventually agreed to go along with the idea. He had a few pictures he thought he could use to introduce Ama to them. Matt felt better about leaving. They now had a firm pact to include family in their relationship. He looked forward to being home in a couple of hours to pack, with enough time to prepare for his trip to meet Marie and Alan. He often missed them, particularly in the empty house that had not seemed so big when they were growing up. He was looking forward to seeing them and having some fun together while sharing news.

Chapter Twenty-eight

The weeks after Andrew's accident and recovery flew by with the start of the summer semester, which was packed with different projects as well as goodbyes as some students ended their studies. Ama realised that it was a changing scenario. Matt had an additional few months as a classmate with Ama before he was done as well. Then Ama would be on her own, making new friends as other students replaced those she had met before. This was to be followed by her internship and research for her Doctorate. Her decision to complete some of this at Matt's clinic was accepted. The rest would be done at a health clinic arranged by her tutor.

Ama had been shaken by her son's accident and recognised how quickly things could change. This unsettled her for some time as she worried about being so far away.

She had checked up on him a few times each week until he was fully recovered and back to work. Maybe his experience also had a positive impact on him; he seemed to his mother to be the son she remembered before the concerns of adulthood and marriage had taken him in an almost different direction. Susan had at times been the babysitter on the few occasions that she was asked, and since the accident, the couples seemed to be closer, from what Ama heard.

Jon was still a bit on the outside in the sibling interaction being the youngest and always a bit like the third wheel. He was also still away from the country, in the closing stages of his studies, seeking the qualifications that would help him find his way in the world. Ama had set up a monthly family chat online, and they had all decided that a family reunion/holiday would be a good idea for August. Jon should be finished with his studies for the time being, and they all felt it was time that Ama came home for a visit, to which she agreed. Nothing much had been said about Evans in all of this, but she got the impression that he was happy, and there was nothing to stop them from being family, while not being married.

Matt and Ama saw each other in shared classes, had regular late-night phone conversations, and met at least once every week for dinner, days out for a walk, or other outdoor activity, and different events. Amidst their busy schedules, Matt invited Ama for a second visit to his home when his children were there over a long holiday weekend in June. They had agreed that their relationship was one they wanted to preserve and share with their families, whatever form it would take. The situation with Ama may be a bit different and somewhat challenging but she was now more hopeful, with the signs of healing in her family, that it would all work out in the way God intended. Her faith in this regard remained firmly in place. She would take one day at a time.

Ama remained in contact with Jennie, hearing about her new experiences and how much she was enjoying life in what was likely to be her new home. There was a plan to return just to finalise arrangements with her family home. She had not yet made up her mind to sell and had decided that leasing would be best. She would find a real estate company to take over the management of it while she was abroad. Ama exchanged regular emails with her friend and they had long phone conversations every few weeks.

In one of those conversations, Jennie shared news of a Christmas wedding, sounding elated with the prospect of marriage, something she had not considered until now. She believed that she had met the right person. She and Ama joked that it had taken her long enough, but they both agreed it was worth the wait.

In their phone chats, Jennie and Ama shared updates about their new relationships, both expressing feelings that they had not expected at this stage in their lives. Matt and Ama had not reached the stage for any conversation about marriage. Ama still did not know if that was a possibility for her, but she would celebrate with her best friend in the world, who had always been there for her. Ama was looking forward to being there, escorted by Matt, and was happy to be the matron of honour.

Ama had had a packed week just before the long weekend at Matt's home. That was not unusual, as she pushed ahead with her programme, really enjoying the added dimensions of practical work that she did individually and with a study group. Her work had not left her with much time to worry about her meeting with Matt's children in person, and most importantly, their meeting her. She had heard a lot about them, filling in the bits that Matt could not say and felt like she knew them. How they would feel about her, however, was the one thing she could not prepare herself for. She knew how important it was for them to like her and felt a wave of anxiety weaving its way through her as she prepared herself for the visit the next day.

Ama and Matt had met briefly that evening before agreeing that a good night's sleep was the best idea before the early departure for the weekend ahead. The children had travelled to their old home the day before, with Martha reporting on their safe arrival. She was no doubt enjoying having them at home, a reminder of earlier days. Ama had also not yet talked to Matt about her summer trip home, and it was another thing on her mind just before she finally fell asleep.

Ama was excited as she left her apartment the next day, expecting to see Matt just driving up to meet her in the parking area outside her apartment building. She loved how he was always on time, never leaving her to wait for him. She guessed it was a sign of how much he appreciated her, but she also knew that this was Matt's way. He was generally focussed on what he had to do and seemed to have similar respect for everyone. She liked that about him.

Ama felt happy in the coolness of the morning amidst the brilliance of the sunshine. She felt that this was the greatest part of summertime – sunshine without it being too hot.

She smiled broadly seeing Matt as he parked nearest

the building and got out of the car to walk briskly towards her. He walked tall with brisk strides – this handsome man of her dreams. She almost gave a chuckle just as he reached her and enveloped her in a hug, as though he had not just seen her just last evening. Then she did just as she saw the reflection of similar emotion in his expression. Then, they laughed at the same time, recognising the mutual glee and looking forward to their time together.

In that moment, Matt and Ama were in the shared world of their creation – a lovely day when they were together. They felt young and carefree as they settled into the vehicle and drove off, ready to embrace the new experience that the day would bring.

Matt was convinced that his children would love Ama, even though it might take them a bit of time. He had no concerns about that. Ama was hopeful that the meeting with Alan and Marie would go well. She felt that she had had a lot of experience with young people and that it should be okay despite the tiniest element of anxiety that she dismissed. She knew that was a bit different from her other encounters with young people. This mattered more personally, but her understanding of their needs, particularly in Alan's case, would be helpful, she thought.

The view from the window was always so pleasant for Ama. She enjoyed leaving the city and going out into the changing countryside as they drove through different counties to arrive finally at Matt's home. They had not stopped, as Ama told Matt that she was fine with the long drive. Matt had driven more slowly through more picturesque places, and they had shared the drinks that

Ama had packed. The trip had seemed shorter this time.

Conversation between them had flowed as it usually did, with some moments of quiet that felt peaceful and almost breath taking in a different sense. At those times, they looked ahead with shared looks at the other. Everything was good in the world they shared.

Chapter Twenty-nine

Matt had the usual welcoming party as he drove up to the entrance of his home. On this occasion, though, there was a call to alert others that he had arrived, and out the door came a young woman that Ama immediately recognised as Marie. She looked briefly at Matt and prepared herself for the first meeting with his daughter.

Marie was a slim-built girl of average height, wearing denim shorts and a loosely-fitted jumper in bright colours. She literally dashed across the distance between the door and the parking area where her father had stopped his vehicle, closing in on him with a shriek of delight. It was obvious that she adored her dad, and the feeling appeared to be mutual as he laughingly and lovingly embraced her. It had been just a few weeks since he had visited them, but Marie was obviously happy to be home.

Matt released himself gently from his daughter's embrace to draw her attention to Ama, who had remained seated in the vehicle, not wanting to interrupt this reunion. She felt unexpectedly shy too, and suddenly conscious of this situation that was totally new to her. All of what had been happening over the last two plus years was new, she acknowledged, as she responded to Matt, who opened the door where Ama still sat, extending his arm in encouragement.

Marie stood, also looking a bit shy herself, meeting her father's girlfriend. She had never before been introduced to any woman her father liked but had thought, from what her father had told her and her brother, that she would like Ama. When Ama looked across at her, their eyes met, and they both seemed to realise almost simultaneously that they were not unalike. Ama, at that moment, decided that Marie could have been one of her students, and she was quite able to manage such situations.

Ama reached across with both arms extended towards Marie with a friendly, inviting smile and was taken by surprise when Marie quickly closed the gap and put her arms around her in a spontaneously friendly embrace. Ama accepted the tight squeeze that lasted a few seconds before she was released. She felt enchanted by Marie's broad smile and responded to her almost childlike and slightly breathless greeting.

"Hello, Ama! It's nice to meet you! Dad told us everything about you!"

"I've heard a lot about you too," Ama replied. "I'm very happy to meet you as well."

Matt and Ama shared glances, and she saw his expression that showed his pleasure in seeing them together. He did not seem surprised by Marie's welcome towards Ama.

The bags had already been taken into the house by the young boy Ama recognised from her last visit. In all the excitement, she had to work on remembering his name – yes, David. As the previous time, he was beaming, happy to welcome Dr Matt and his lady friend.

Everyone turned to walk towards the door, and Ama got ready to greet Alan, who was standing there waiting for them. She would have recognised him even without the benefits of photos she had seen. He stood quietly, looking so much like Matt. His expression was somewhat neutral, but she saw something more in his eyes as he prepared to greet his father and Ama. There was no exchange of any physical sign of affection, but Ama saw the hint of a smile that lighted up his face as he focussed on his father. This reaction was immediate before his gaze shifted to Ama walking next to his father, and he raised his arm to greet her politely. Ama expressed her pleasure with a firm and friendly clasping of Alan's hand, a broad smile directed at him as she said how pleased she was to meet him.

Coming up from behind, Marie teased her brother with a giggle about his gentlemanly approach before they all walked inside.

Reflecting on the greeting afterwards in her room, the same as the one she had previously, Ama thought it was lovely how Matt's two children complemented each other. Alan, with his social communication needs, was fully accepted by his family, and Marie's joyful and spritely engagement with those around her was a good foil for his demeanour. Marie had made the transition from a few years of struggle without her mother, and Ama realised that this could also have been in part a response to her father's own difficulty coping with Alan's autism and learning how to meet the needs of his two children. The work he had done on himself and for his children had definitely borne fruit for their family. Both young people seemed quite balanced and positive about their lives. Matt could be as proud of himself as he obviously was of them.

Both young people brought more life to the home environment, and they were joined at times by friends who had heard Marie and Alan were at home. They were young people who were at early stages of career of just finishing college like Marie, mostly also visiting family over the long holiday weekend. Their presence brought out a different side to Matt that Ama was seeing for the first time. It was not that he was different, really, but she was now seeing how he responded as a dad, patiently listening but, in some ways, exerting a slightly firm hand in helping them to manoeuvre situations within the household itself and in decisions related to their interaction in their friendship groups.

Matt was proud to see how independent they had become, with Alan now living in young adult accommodations with a job in IT and a girlfriend. The setting was designed for supporting young people with autism with the challenges of career and social life while helping them to develop that much-needed independence apart from family and home. Marie was accustomed to living within a university dormitory, managing her studies and internship programmes. She had decided to add a degree in Psychology to previous work in Art and Photography, which she had insisted was still something she enjoyed but more as a hobby now.

The weekend passed too quickly, with some conversation focussed on travelling abroad and perhaps to Ama's tropical island home. They agreed to talk about it in the weeks ahead and put a plan in motion. Marie had asked for Ama's email address and mobile phone number, and Ama looked forward to hearing from her. Ama had been able to engage Alan in conversation on more than one occasion. She was always interested in hearing young people talk about their hopes for the future, and Alan was quite willing to talk about his career interests and even a little about Emily, who he enjoyed being with quite a lot.

In a late evening stroll on their last day, Matt and Ama agreed that the weekend had gone as well as or even better than they had hoped. Matt had driven Alan and Ama to the train station that afternoon, and they would each take taxis – Alan to his apartment and Marie to her university not too far away. They would drive back to the city in the morning with lots of time for them to be ready for work the next day. Matt only had a couple of classes that week, but Ama had a packed schedule including group work and direct work as part of her practicum. This was a short semester, but she knew how important it was for her to complete it successfully. She did not want to have anything flow over to the next year or to have to repeat anything when she wanted to have this trip home, hopefully with Matt and his children joining her at some stage. She was looking forward to all of it.

Chapter Thirty

"Please prepare for landing!"

Ama reached her seat just in time to follow the instructions, buckling her seat belt for the last time before she would be home. It had been only one year since she had been abroad but it seemed like a lifetime had passed. So much had happened, so many things had changed. She had checked in one large suitcase with just a few personal items of her own but mostly gifts for her children and grandchildren. She had a carry-on case with her laptop stored in the overhead locker. She had occupied the nine-hours mostly reading and intermittently watching at a film. It had not been the most comfortable journey, seated between two other travellers, and she looked forward stretching her legs.

She thought then of saying goodbye to Matt that morning at the airport. He had been a bit anxious before having to see her off, before recalling that he and his children would soon be joining her. They had thought it better not to travel together, giving Ama time to settle in with her family and avoiding the need to establish too early how serious their relationship was. Ama was not looking forward to meeting Evans, particularly not having heard from him or what he had been doing. She was a bit concerned about the attention that would be given to Matt and his children but decided that it would have to work itself out. They were travelling the week after and staying at a city hotel. She would focus on enjoying the holiday with family and showing Matt, Alan, and Marie around. It should be fine.

Ama inhaled the air even as he basked in the last bit of sunshine just before dusk. She was expecting Andrew to meet her and looked around for him. Immigration had not taken long despite the crowd during this time of year so she expected to have to wait a bit – Andrew was likely to factor in some additional time from the time of landing. He was never one to be early or even on time, she thought of her elder son.

With her cases propped up at her feet, Ama looked around at the people greeting and saying goodbye to relatives and friends. This friendly atmosphere was home and Ama realised how much she had missed it although she had not had a lot of time to dwell on it. Ama was almost startled when a slight tap on her shoulder alerted her to Andrew's presence.

"Hi, Mother!" he said with his familiar grin.

"Andrew! You're here! I didn't even see you drive up!" Ama responded, examining her son before embracing him. She remembered the scare she had had just a couple of months ago. Thank God, here he was, as well as ever, she thought, with a grateful smile.

"I'm in the car park, not wanting to be driving around in case you were delayed."

"*Hmm,* things have changed." Ama laughed at him. This was definitely a more responsible Andrew.

It was a calm and pleasant drive to Andrew and Amelia's house. She had decided to stay there a couple of days before going over to Susan's house where she was likely to stay for the rest of her visit. It would not make sense to stay in rented accommodation for such a short time. When Jon arrived, he would stay in their old home with his father. Despite some uncomfortableness related to her separation from Evans, Ama was happy to be here with her family. She believed they had grown past the initial drama around its occurrence and they would be able to celebrate being family. She had told them about a

friend and his family joining them and was likely to talk more about it to them individually.

The week was passing very smoothly, with Ama occupied for much of her time shared between her children, and individual or group outings including the dinner they had at a favourite restaurant. By that time, Jon was also in the country celebrating his success in final exams. Of course, Evans had been there and their greeting and interaction had been cordial and even friendly at times. She had noted how well he looked, and even happy which reassured her somewhat.

It was the day before she expected Matt and his children and she was lounging at Susan's home. The young family had gone out, running some errands including check-ups for the children and Ama was using her time alone to catch up with university notices and emails from Jennie. From the distance, she saw the mailman passing and decided to check the mailbox. She had put Susan's address as her mailing address and would often be told about mail that arrived for her.

Ama looked through the three envelopes and picked out the one with her name. She did not recognise the sender as she opened it, sitting on the porch as she did so. Reading through the contents she was taken totally by surprise. It was a typed letter from Evans! They had not really talked to each other since she left the country, both realising that it had not helped with any attempt at real conversation ending in an argument. Chatting about mundane things e.g. during the family dinner including others was fine through a mutual interest in not upsetting their children and maintaining as much of a family life as possible. The children appeared to have made a pact about not sharing news about the other or maybe this would also be news to them.

Ama realised that she needed some time to digest the news that Evans was planning to go abroad to join a woman. During the last two years or so of their marriage, she had heard about her from Evans himself when they had started communicating via email and then WhatsApp. He had then dismissed her as a friend, someone he knew long before they were married. She had left the country travelling across the world to marry a pen pal.

Evans may have had feelings for her but had not made them clear to her during the time they had spent together, sharing some similar interests. Ama could not recall him telling her how they had reconnected but her husband had died leaving the property that she continued to manage. They had not had any children so she was basically as alone as before, despite some friendships and interactions with her late husband's relatives. Now, he was going to join her. *Amazing,* Ama thought.

In a typewritten one-page letter, Evan outlined his concern about her reaction to his plans for the future. He wanted her agreement that she would not oppose any steps he would need to take for him to be able to marry again.

Ama remained dumbfounded for quite a few minutes. She had not expected this and was still seated there in some reflection when her daughter returned home with her husband and two children. Ama wondered if she should say anything and then decided that it was his story to tell. She thought of Matt and his children's arrival the next day and considered what the impact of all of this would be on their own children. True they were adults but this was still a lot to manage, she thought to herself.

Ama decided that it may be best not to say anything until the end of this holiday. She would leave Evans to talk to them about his plans. She would share her feelings of support for him and would eventually be free to talk about her plans for the future, though not yet decided.

Ama realised at that moment that she had released the breath that she had held in for so long. She hoped then that Evans had found his happily ever after which could only come with someone who was able to love, honour and respect him, accepting him as he is. Ama knew then that she had not been able to do that and therefore could not inspire in him the love and acceptance she had always desired and needed.

EPILOGUE

Ama was back home to celebrate a wedding and a new life. It was a short hike up the hill overlooking the ocean, Ama's favourite place in the world – mountains populated with a forest of trees in rich bloom and the stretch of open sea as far as the eye can see.

This is where her heart remains, shared by a man and a family she had not expected but seemed to have been designed for her.

First, to reach the top, Ama had time to reflect, as she had done on so many occasions before this day. She thought about all that had happened over the last three years and connected to all that had gone before in her life to that point.

Ama again saw herself feeling confident and at ease as she had walked across the stage to the applause of the packed auditorium. It had been almost two years since her visit home during the summer after Andrew's accident. Family and friends had gathered to celebrate the graduation of loved ones. She knew that her family was also in the audience – her children and spouses, and Matt and his children, with one spouse and soon-to-be spouse. Evans was already living his new life by then and was not present. Poised for the photograph, she reached across with a handshake for the Chancellor and to receive her

Doctoral certificate, smiling broadly.

So much more had happened. She knew that she had felt freer meeting Matt and his two children in her home setting after finding out about Evans' plans. They had had a great time. Matt's and her children seemed to become instant friends even Alan seemed to develop an immediate connection with Jon despite Alan being the older one, he responded well to Jon, almost like a big brother. Marie fitted right in with the children and with their parents.

Evans was rarely around when the entire family gathered, but he and Matt had met at a dinner. Matt and his children had spent ten days with daily excitement and trips to appreciate the beauty of Ama's homeland, including the beaches and hikes through the green forests. They also enjoyed the friendly, outgoing people, the music, and the food that characterised social events.

Once Matt had heard about Evans' plans, he felt freed from the pressure of Ama's previous marriage and felt more able to share his hopes and dreams for their future together. They could hardly believe how well their families were blending.

Ama had not had a strong bond with her siblings, but she sought always to include them, as their family was otherwise quite small. She had invited her sister to the last family dinner and visited once with her. She had shared the news with her sister who lived abroad. Her little world had, over the last four years, expanded in a way that she could never have hoped.

Matt and Ama had travelled for Jennie's wedding. Ama was the maid of honour and was happy to be there for the friend who had supported her so well over the years. She was elated about seeing her as the star of her own happy-ever-after story.

Ama had worked hard to succeed with her university programme, spending the last year on her research, which included six months working as a practitioner in the well-being clinic. This had expanded in terms of service to include other therapeutic approaches. Marie had also decided to pursue postgraduate work in Psychotherapy, deciding that this was the direction she wanted to take. She had met Matt's latest veterinary assistant during the year she interned there, and they seemed to be a match made in heaven. They were both prepared to carry on the work Matt had started so he could pursue the life he wanted with Ama.

At the end of the dinner celebrating her graduation, Matt had gone down on one knee to propose marriage to Ama. She had felt so overwhelmed with emotion as she looked around at the faces of the people she loved most in the world. She had almost forgotten to say yes. It was the most heartfelt moment when she did. Ama knew then that being swept into marriage on a wave of youthful fantasy was significantly different from getting married to the man you know you will love and cherish for the rest of your life, and who would love and cherish you right back. She looked forward to them continuing to climb mountains together.

Ama stood waiting at the spot where they now had designs for a home with enough space that was ideal for their well-being centre, almost a duplicate of what Matt had left behind to begin a life with her. She looked back at the group trailing her steps, welcoming them – her husband, her family, two generations after her. She was finally home.